THE SYSTEMS OF M. R. SHURNAS

THE SYSTEMS OF M. R. SHURNAS

A Novel

by

DAVID NEMEC

RIVERRUN PRESS   JOHN CALDER

NEW YORK   LONDON

First published in the United States 1985 by
Riverrun Press Inc.,
1170 Broadway,
New York, NY 10001

And in Great Britain 1985 by
John Calder (Publishers) Ltd.,
18 Brewer Street,
London W1R 4AS

Library of Congress Cataloging in Publication Data

Nemec, David.
  The systems of M.R. Shurnas.
  I. Title.
PS3564.E4797S9   1985   813'.54   83-19198
ISBN 0-8667-6011-3 (pbk.)

Nemec, David 1985

British Library Cataloguing in Publication Data

Nemec, David
  The systems of M.R. Shurnas.
  I. Title
  813'.54[F]   PS3564.E/
ISBN 0-7145-4022-6 Pbk

SUBSIDISED BY THE
Arts Council
OF GREAT BRITAIN

Printed and bound in Great Britain
by Heffers Printers Limited, Cambridge.

"What we all dread is a maze
with no center..."
CHESTERTON

CHAPTER ONE

In the middle of his first-round tournament match M.R. Shurnas walked off the court. As he went down the cinder path to the clubhouse, he passed a group of players who were clustered around the drinking fountain. All of them seemed to be smiling. At first Shurnas could not make himself believe they were smiling at him, then he could not make himself believe they were not. He looked down. Since he was righthanded his tennis racket should have been in his right hand, but it was in his left.

Shurnas could not think how the racket had got into his left hand. On the surface it was a small thing, but it was the small things that led to confusion if you didn't keep on top of them. He could have switched the racket to his left hand when he left the court so that his right hand would be free in case there was trouble. But it hadn't been that kind of situation. Before walking off the court he hadn't said anything, and his opponent—the man's name was on the tournament draw sheet, but Shurnas, a seeded player, hadn't bothered to look at it before the match—had made no move to stop him.

It was a hot July afternoon. In the clubhouse Shurnas put some coins into the soda machine and pushed a button. He got an orange drink instead of the Coke he was expecting, but it might not have been the machine's fault. He had used his left hand to push the button, and it was trembling a little. Somehow his tennis racket had got from his left hand back into his right. Probably when he'd opened the clubhouse door. And yet Shurnas thought he remembered putting the coins into the machine with his right hand. Logically, it must have been his right hand. For luck, he always carried his change in the right-hand pocket of his shorts.

All of his movements were beginning to bother him. He tried to avoid doing anything that wasn't absolutely necessary. In the dressing room he sat in front of his locker and stared into it until his hands stopped shaking. It was an old high school trick, but after all these years it still seemed to work. "Think about it," his coach used to say after a losing game. "Don't let yourself feel better until you feel it will never happen again." Back then it had been easy to listen to that sort of advice because you hadn't known that no amount of thinking about things would stop them from happening.

While taking a shower he felt himself grow annoyed by the look the man whose locker was beside his had given him. On his left kneecap he noticed a black and blue mark. The knee itself was a little swollen. He couldn't decide whether the injury had occurred during the match. "It must be age," he thought. And yet when had there been a time when his body had not suffered from one ailment or another?

In leaving the clubhouse he had to pass the table where the tournament director was entering the scores of each match on a large draw sheet. Shurnas was informed that his opponent had been declared the winner of their match by default. When asked for his explanation of events, he asked what his opponent had said and was told it had been alleged that he quit for no reason. Uncertain whether he was more disturbed by the tournament director's use of a word like alleged or his opponent's distortion of his motives, Shurnas was tempted simply to get out of there. But then he heard himself saying, "It's not worth putting a match to your powder in these Mickey Mouse tournaments." For a moment he seemed to see the same expression on the tournament director's face that he had seen earlier on the face of the man whose locker was beside his. It was unnerving to have people persistently look at you as if they couldn't believe you were talking to them.

When Shurnas got to the tennis club in Queens where he worked as a teaching pro, both of the other pros were on the courts giving lessons. One of them, a college player who was only working at the club for the summer, looked up when he saw Shurnas enter the courts and asked how his match had gone. "A real bitch," Shurnas said. "They didn't have any linesmen and the guy I played took advantage of it."

There was a lot more Shurnas could have said, but he sensed that the girl who ran the desk at the club was standing behind him, as if waiting for a moment to interrupt. Turning he saw, not the girl, who he was positive had been there when he began to speak, but the manager of the club. The manager had once been a ranked player in the East but was now in his fifties. Nevertheless he made everyone who came to him for a teaching pro's job play a match with him. Unless they understood they were supposed to lose they were not hired.

Having overheard Shurnas's remark to the college player, the manager said, "Whenever I ran into a cheat on calls, I just cheated him right back." Shurnas started to say that wasn't tennis, but then he realized the manager was telling him he would have to cover for the rest of the afternoon for the college player who had taught his lessons for him while he was in the tournament. Although he had expected this, Shurnas still felt a child's sense of being punished. In the small room behind the pro shop that he and the other pros used as a dressing room he ate a candy bar for quick energy, then stood awhile in front of the soda machine before he remembered that he'd had an orange drink after the tournament. Pleased that he still hadn't had the one Coke to which he limited himself each day, he reached in the pocket of his shorts and counted his change with his fingertips. He was a nickel short. He tried not to take this to mean anything and borrowed a nickel from one of the club members he knew by sight but not by name.

Later he was astonished by how hard he was hitting shots to the woman who was his last lesson of the day. He didn't actually notice this during the lesson itself, but afterward, when he went to pick up the balls, he saw that almost all of them were behind her. Clearly this was because the woman had been overpowered by his shots. As the two of them went around the court gathering the balls, the woman appeared to be trying not to perspire. True, her face was red, but it was perfectly dry. Once, when she straightened after bending for a ball, she ran her hands over her hips to smooth down her dress. Shurnas, who made it a strict rule never to associate with female club members but at the same time had had affairs with several of them, noticed how careful she was still being not to perspire. When they had collected all the balls he offered to buy her a soda.

Because the woman was one of the college player's pupils, Shurnas hadn't listened when she mentioned her name at the beginning of the lesson. Now he tried to think of ways to get her to repeat it. After getting a Coke for her and some kind of juice drink for himself, he said, "You know, I'm sorry, but I didn't catch your last name." He hoped that would induce her to tell him her full name, but all she said was "Turner." Calling her Mrs. Turner, Shurnas waited to see if she would correct him either by saying she wasn't married or else by telling him to call her by her first name. For a few moments, looking for a place to sit down, she said nothing. Then she said, "Do we have to stay out on the courts? Isn't there someplace more comfortable?"

Shurnas looked around himself. They seemed to be the only ones left at the club; it was past six o'clock and the girl who ran the desk had gone home; also it was Saturday, and while the club did not officially close until the courts were too dark for play, on Saturday evenings there was seldom anyone around. "We're a tennis club, not a social club," the manager had informed Shurnas when he was hired.

The sauna was deserted. Upon entering it, Shurnas tossed a pail of water over the rocks. Beginning to perspire lightly now, the woman took off everything but her bra and panties.

"Will anyone come in here?" she asked.

Shurnas felt that others given an opening like that would have said knowingly, "Just you and I," and he resented that he was not allowed to do anything more than shrug.

The woman said, "I feel so silly with all my clothes off when you're still dressed." She sat on the bottom ledge of the wood platform. In a moment she moved to the upper ledge and lay down. Shurnas took off his shoes, socks and shirt. He pretended to be having trouble undoing the zipper of his shorts. Something was making him uneasy. He decided it was not having suggested they take a shower before getting started. Then he decided it wasn't that at all but the fact that the woman was doing this even though he hadn't given her a good lesson. He remembered the anxious look on her face as she missed one shot of his after another. Once a ball had struck her solidly in the knee. He looked now at her knee to see if it had left a mark. In glancing down he noticed that the bruise on his own knee seemed larger. Suddenly he realized that the woman, without really looking to see what she was doing, was helping him undo the zipper of his shorts. The fingers on both her hands had many rings on them. Watching her fingers fumble over the zipper, Shurnas remembered the way they had glinted in the bright sunlight during the lesson. Then he remembered that his opponent in the tournament had worn a ring. Attached to his shorts the man had also worn a small pouch filled with dirt which he sprinkled on his racket handle between points, as if to keep from losing his grip.

Shurnas stepped out of his shorts. Then he watched the

woman rather shyly watch him remove his jockstrap. Perspiring heavily now, she fell back on her elbows. "It gets hot in here, doesn't it," she said. Infected with some of her shyness, Shurnas hoped she would not mistakenly surmise, when he started for the door of the sauna, that he had to urinate.

There were three shower cubicles outside the sauna. Shurnas entered one of them and closed the door behind him even though no one was around. While soaping himself he discovered he really did have to urinate. He had never felt entirely secure urinating in the shower, but there seemed no alternative now that he was standing behind a closed door.

The woman still had her bra and panties on when he returned to the sauna. Raising herself on one elbow, she said, "Would you be satisfied if I just gave you head?" Her tone made it a question, but without waiting from his answer she took his penis in one hand while the other brushed the hair back from her face. Shurnas stood watching her get into a kneeling position on the platform that left them still too far apart for her mouth to reach him. After a while he knelt on the platform himself. This was better but made his bruised knee hurt. Kneeling there, he noticed that someone had carved the initials "R.T." on the wall a few inches above the woman's head.

His opponent's behavior in the tournament was still on his mind. Several times Shurnas had hit serves that were unquestionably long only to have the man sharply return them and then claim the point when Shurnas made no attempt to play the returns. When Shurnas threatened to call the tournament director if this practice continued, the man had said, "I call everything on my side of the court, you call everything on yours. Sometimes we'll both make mistakes, but that's the price you have to pay for playing in these Mickey Mouse tournaments where they're too cheap to hire linesmen." Only now did Shurnas realize that the man had been the source of the phrase "Mickey Mouse tournaments" that he had used in speaking to the tournament director. This knowledge made him too nervous to concentrate on the woman's efforts to arouse him.

The initials on the wall had been carved very crudely as if they were done by someone in a hurry. The woman could have put them there herself on one of her earlier visits to the sauna. Her name could be Rhonda Turner. Or Rose. Or Rachel. Shurnas, feeling the woman begin to massage his balls lightly, decided that of the three he could least afford for her name to be Rose. Then one of her rings scratched him and he made a mild sound of discomfort. She made an answering sound. In a moment she raised her head and said she really wanted him inside her.

Because he had known this request would be made eventually, Shurnas began removing her panties without saying anything. The woman said, "But please, you'll have to be careful because I didn't bring my kit." Shurnas, misunderstanding, thought she had said kid. This struck him as so arch that he couldn't stop himself from frowning. The woman, as he had been afraid she would, became very solicitous as if worried that he found her unappealing.

His erection abandoning him, Shurnas sat down beside her and watched perspiration fall from her face and form a pool on the floor in front of her while she tried to excite him again with her hand. Finally she said if it made such a difference to him he could come inside her without worrying, it was nearly time for her period anyway. Awhile later she said, "What would you say if I told you I'd had the menopause?" Her choice of words baffled him. Was the word "the" really necessary? As he mulled this over he felt her take his hand and place it between her legs. The moisture there was largely perspiration that had dribbled down from her face, but it enabled him routinely to alternate penetrating her with his middle finger and index finger.

The woman murmured something. He just nodded. Then

7

she said something about wanting to take lessons from him from now on instead of the college player. "You're much more patient with me." Having believed all along that her only reason for doing this was because he was a tennis pro, Shurnas wondered as he moved forward over her if she had also had an affair with the college player. Once he had glided into her, he remembered how matted her pubic hair had looked when he removed her panties. He reached around her back and unhooked the clasp on her bra, noting that her breasts looked as if they belonged on the body of a much taller woman. Before coming he made movements to signal her it was about to happen—in part so she would have time to stop him in case she had any last-second thoughts about him doing it inside her but more to inform her that he at least was still awake. Her eyes were closed and she lay rigidly still on her back. Shurnas's thighs slapping against hers were the only sound in the sauna.

Later in the evening he dropped into a bar in Lower Manhattan that was on the edge of the SoHo district but was not frequented much by artists. Most of its patrons were athletes who played on the various New York professional teams and Shurnas thought he recognized one of the Yankees' pitchers. Sitting at the bar, he was himself recognized by several people who knew him from the days when he had been the city public courts champion. One of them told him about a party. Shurnas, who already knew of two other parties that night, dutifully copied the address on the cover of a book of matches which he later loaned to someone at the bar and did not bother to get back. He ordered a hamburg, french fries and a beer—none of which he finished. When a man who had once been a doubles partner of his came in and took the empty stool beside him, Shurnas realized he at last had someone with whom he could share his experience in the tournament that day but instead he found himself describing the incident with the woman in the sauna. He omitted many of the details—

including his having seen her initials on the wall—but still felt he was taking too long to tell the story. He stopped in the middle and ordered another beer, although the first one still sat in front of him unfinished. Aware that the man had started a story of his own, Shurnas looked at his watch and rose. Hesitating only long enough to drink as much of the second beer as he had of the first so that the picture of the two glasses beside each other would not look too incongruous, he said, "Great seeing you again. We have to play soon. Call me." As he headed for the door, marveling at his hurry to get out of the place, he took a deep breath.

Outside the street was wet as if there had just been a cloud-burst. But before he could think it was about time they had a little rain, he noticed that the water was coming from an open hydrant on down the street; already deep puddles had formed at each intersection. One of the parties he knew about was in a loft building not far from the bar. Moving in the direction of the building, Shurnas counted the steps it took him to cover each block. When the first three blocks had all taken the same number of steps, he began lengthening his strides so that the remaining blocks would take fewer. In a while he grew aware of a dull pain below his injured knee and shortened his strides again. The pain went away, but the next block he traveled required exactly the same number of steps as the first three. He wondered to himself if the city was really so geometrically perfect or if rather he wasn't just trying to make it perfect. Around then it occurred to him that in keeping count of his steps he had not been paying attention to puddles. His shoes were soaked. Luckily, it was a warm night. "No harm done," Shurnas told himself. He didn't worry about his health nearly as much in the summer.

Upon arriving at the building where the party was, he had to wait a long time for the elevator. When it came some people who had arrived after he did jostled him aside and got on ahead of him. Shurnas said nothing, but on the ride up he stood smiling numbly at no one in particular. The elevator door opened on a long dimly lit room where the floor shone like a bowling alley and voices carried deep and sepulchral as in a cave. Shurnas made for a table at the far end of the room where some bottles of wine and plates of cheese had been set out. As he poured himself a glass of wine, a woman came over and held her glass out for a refill. "Hello, I'm Mary," she said. Without waiting for Shurnas to introduce himself, she started telling him about a movie she had seen earlier in the evening. In a few minutes two men joined their conversation; it turned out that both of them had seen the same movie a few days before but thought it sounded, from Mary's description, as if some scenes had been left out of the print they saw. "It happens a lot now," one of the men said. "Everything's change for the sake of change."

Panicked the three of them were going to turn to him for his opinion, Shurnas sought the phone. As he was dialing a number, a woman in a blue wraparound skirt came running over. "I'll make it quick," she said, taking the phone out of his hand. For several minutes Shurnas listened to her argue with someone over which train to take to East Hampton the following morning. Finally he had the phone to himself. Since he'd left his address book in his locker at the club, he could only call the numbers, he had memorized. When he got one of the women he knew at home, he talked of other things awhile before asking her if she wanted company for the night. They agreed that he would come over around one o'clock, by which time the movie she wanted to see on TV would be over.

Shurnas decided to wile away the hours until one o'clock at the other party he knew about. Rather than wait for the elevator he was going to leave the building by the stairs, but he couldn't find them. Every door he opened seemed to lead to another part of the loft. As he started toward the only door he hadn't tried, it opened on its own and he saw it was the elevator. He got in. Before the door closed the woman named Mary stuck her head in and asked him to hold the elevator a moment. In a while she and the two men who had seen the same movie all got in. Shurnas gathered they were now a threesome, but when the elevator reached the ground floor Mary shook hands quickly with each of the men and got off alone. Disconcerted, Shurnas himself nearly did not get off the elevator in time; the door was starting to close before he made his move.

When he got outside the building, Mary was standing in the middle of the street. At first he thought she was looking for a cab, but as he started to walk away he heard her say something. Turning, he watched her approach him. Even as she started telling him she lived only a few doors down the street, she took his arm as if there was no question that he would want to go home with her. At the corner Shurnas suggested they go to the other party he knew about instead. She appeared to agree, but when he hailed a cab she refused to get into it. "Let's walk," she pleaded. Looking at her, Shurnas wondered whether she knew something about him that he didn't.

They wound up in a bar on Spring Street where they had to wait half an hour for a table. She told him not to order any food because she had lots back at her place, then ordered a spinach salad for herself. By the time their drinks arrived she was holding his hand on top of the table and drawing little circles with her finger on his palm. She asked if he was an earth sign but did not question him further when he said he wasn't. Shurnas said the reason his palm was so calloused was because he played a lot of tennis. Before starting on their drinks she insisted they touch glasses in a silent toast, then excused herself to go to the restroom. Puzzled whether it was his not being an earth sign or the condition of his hand that had made up her mind against him, Shurnas took some money out of his pocket, laid it beside his untouched drink and left the bar.

There were some more puddles on the street. Shurnas

looked to see if another hydrant was open, but this time the water was coming from a hose a man was using to wash his car. Shurnas found a cab and told the driver to take him to the second party. The driver wanted to know if Shurnas meant Greenwich Street or Greenwich Avenue. Shurnas said he hadn't known there was a difference, but the important part of the address wasn't Greenwich anyway—it was Jane Street. The driver claimed to know where Jane Street was, but when Shurnas saw they were headed downtown instead of toward the Village, he told the driver to stop the cab and got out without paying. He was all prepared for an argument, but the driver merely said, "Have a good evening," and drove away.

Shurnas walked a block or two, then caught a second cab. The driver, a young woman wearing jeans and an army fatigue cap, dropped him right in front of the building on the corner of Jane and Greenwich where the party was. Shurnas invited her to come to it with him, and when she said she couldn't because Saturday was her biggest night for fares, he scribbled the address on a piece of paper which he handed her along with his tip. "In case things get slow," he murmured, but when she smiled at him he quickly looked away.

Entering the lobby of the building, Shurnas had an immediate sense that he was in the wrong place. Then he understood the source of his confusion: the lobby had been painted a different color since he'd last been there. The couple who were having the party were his oldest friends, but he hadn't seen them in over a year. Shurnas supposed the rift had developed because they were still friendly with his ex-wife and felt torn maintaining a friendship with him as well. When they had called his answering service and left a message telling him about the party, he had assumed they were inviting him only because she couldn't make it.

Since it was nearly eleven o'clock, a sizeable crowd was present. Shurnas didn't see his hosts but discovered, while

12

searching for them in the various rooms of the apartment, that he knew almost everyone there. A joint was being passed. Shurnas took it and handed it along, after taking a drag, to a young woman standing nearby. She was part of a group listening to a child tell a joke that Shurnas hadn't heard since his own childhood. At first Shurnas thought the child was a boy, but when he got close enough to hear its voice he was no longer sure. "Pete and Repeat went down to the lake," the child was saying. "Pete fell in and drowned. Who was left?" When someone said, "Repeat," the child giggled and began the joke all over again. Shurnas did not know whether he was more amazed that people were listening to the child or that the child was there at all.

In the kitchen he ran into a man who had known him before he became a tennis pro. The man asked him if he was still teaching in junior high school. Shurnas had to think for a minute before he realized the man had him mixed up with someone else who had once been friendly with the two of them. "You're thinking of Louis," Shurnas said, then realized he had mixed things up a little himself, because this man was Louis and the other man's name was something like Dean or Don.

Annoyed, the man started to correct Shurnas, but a woman came into the kitchen and said, "As long as you boys are here, make yourselves useful." She opened the refrigerator and handed them each a dish of dip. Since he and the man had nothing else to talk about, Shurnas swiftly carried his dish into the next room and deposited it on a table amid some other dishes of dip, raw vegetables and the like. On the corner of the table were two joints. Fleetingly Shurnas considered snatching them and putting them in his pocket, but he didn't. He was among friends here; at least he took this to be his reason. There was no thought that it would amount to stealing if he pocketed the joints; it was just that they, like the dip and raw vegetables, were not for private use but for the public enjoyment of everyone at the party.

Awhile later, seeing that the two joints were still on the table, Shurnas debated again whether to take them. But this time his reason for not doing so was because he felt his every action was under close observation by others at the party. Realizing this feeling was perhaps a reaction to the marijuana he had already smoked, he did some knee bends and looked around to see if anyone was watching. None of the people in the room at the moment were familiar to him, but there was a logical explanation for this: he was standing so far away that he only thought they were unfamiliar. He went into the kitchen again. There he saw Jackie. She was wearing the red flapper dress she had bought last summer at a flea market on Canal Street. It had cost her fifty cents, and the color was so garish he had told her she looked as if she was going to a fire.

At the moment she was rinsing out some glasses in the sink. Shurnas watched her from the doorway. Her back was to him. When her hands got too wet to hold the glasses, she seemed about to wipe them on her dress; at least Shurnas took her fluttery movements to be this. Then she reached for a roll of paper towels on the wall rack over the sink. For an instant this view of her made his heart ache. Not only was he seeing Jackie again but he was seeing her in the indecisive state that was his strongest memory of her.

Shurnas went back to the table where he had seen the two joints. They were gone. When he put a cracker into a dish of dip, the cracker broke in two, the piece that remained in the dip sticking straight up in the air like a sail. For the first time it occurred to him that there was marijuana not only in the joints but in the dip as well. He could not imagine that the couple who had invited him to the party would also have invited Jackie unless they had a motive. His own motive for being there was suddenly unclear. In the crowded room he noticed

14

only one person who seemed willing to meet his eyes. But even this glance held no detectable curiosity. Stepping back from the table, he took out a handkerchief and wiped his forehead. Until he performed this action he had not been aware of how warm it had become in the room. As on most occasions when he smoked marijuana, he felt if he closed his eyes he would fall asleep.

In another room he ran into Jackie again. Her eyes when she saw him had so little expression in them that he understood she must have seen him earlier in the kitchen—although he remembered being sure at the time that she hadn't—and forearmed herself against just this moment. He asked her to go home with him. His expectation was that she would either treat the idea as a joke or else take it deadly serious and react by running away from him. When she said all right, he thought at first that she was turning the tables on him so that this time the joke, if you wanted to call it that, would be at his expense; and determined to appear as emotionless as she, he said, "Your place or mine?"

A few minutes later, as they were riding the subway to her apartment on West 82nd Street, it seemed, especially since she was wearing the same dress she had bought at the flea market, that it was still last summer. Though what his mind was to do with all the events that had happened since remained a problem. That Jackie was sitting beside him with the same sullen look she always had whenever they were out in public together, that his own facial features also probably looked a little sullen to anyone watching them, that they had not spoken a word to each other since leaving the party and yet seemed to understand each other's thoughts perfectly—it all made it seem to him as if there had been no interruption between them. "Here we are again," he thought. Happily, the subway was so noisy that their silence could be endured.

From a phone booth in a bar on the corner of Jackie's block, where he had gone while she stopped at the bodega across the street for a quart of milk, he called the woman with whom he had made a date for that night and told her there had been a change in his plans; she said her own had changed too but didn't say how. Shurnas tried not to feel betrayed.

As he and Jackie entered her building, he noticed there was now a black plastic nameplate on her mailbox where her name had merely been printed on a piece of cardboard before. Other items in her life also seemed more embedded. The plaster on her kitchen ceiling was no longer falling, and an air conditioner had been installed in her front window. Under the rather ugly sofa that also served as her bed was a pair of running shoes that gave him a start because he had never known her to do anything more strenuous than clean her apartment. He removed his own shoes and sat on the sofa. He supposed there would soon be a conversation between them and wondered which of them would be the one to start it.

Some moments after he had sat on the sofa Jackie took a seat at the other end of it. He noticed now that her dress seemed more brown than red. So as not to give her an opportunity to accuse him of staring at her, he leafed through a magazine until he heard her tell him to put it down. In the apartment above hers someone dropped an object on the floor; to Shurnas's hypersensitive ears it sounded like a coin. A quarter, he thought. He followed Jackie's eyes for a while without actually catching them looking at him. When he saw how tight the muscles around her mouth were, he began to wish he'd taken the joints he'd seen at the party. Not until she spoke was he going to be able to speak himself. She certainly must have a lot she had been storing up to tell him; why was she taking so long to get started? Shurnas crossed his legs. Eventually he picked up the magazine again but, out of respect for Jackie, at first didn't look at it. Then he found himself looking at it. A cartoon occupied the upper lefthand side of the page the magazine was opened to, but the rest of the page was given over to a

16

story about a couple hunting for an apartment in Manhattan. Their names were Michael and Cecily. Despite feeling himself smile to himself, Shurnas recognized that he was furious. He was frightened that, even though he knew better, he would make some remark to Jackie about the story.

When she got up after a while and went into the bathroom, Shurnas realized he was trying to will her, as long as she was in there anyway, to put in her diaphragm. By this time all the effects of the marijuana he had smoked at the party had worn off. He moved closer to the middle of the sofa but not so close to it that it would be obvious, should Jackie be watching for just this sort of thing, that he had moved. After she returned he crossed his legs again. Abruptly, and in a voice so natural that he was startled, he heard himself say, "Well, how have you been?" For a moment the woman in the magazine story, of which he had read only the first few paragraphs, seemed more real to him than Jackie did.

She talked briefly about what she had been doing lately, but in such general terms that Shurnas, listening closely to her report of her activities, could not remember from one moment to the next what she'd said. Only when she put her head back against the sofa and closed her eyes did he turn and look directly at her. To his surprise, she threw herself into his arms and kissed him with an ease that was so uncharacteristic of her he was immediately aroused. He started to remove her clothes. When she was naked he recognized that there had been yet another change in her life: her breasts, her thighs, indeed, every part of her body was as tanned as her face and arms. Predictably, when he went down on her, she froze up; her head fell back against the sofa again and her eyes closed. For the next several minutes, observing that even the lips of her vagina seemed darker than he remembered them, as if they too had been tanned, he tried various methods to excite her but gave up when she said, "Just do it."

Distracted by a noise soon after entering her, Shurnas raised

17

his head and looked around. Because they hadn't turned out the light, their shadows flitted across the walls of the room. Forgetting the noise in his preoccupation with watching the shadows, he heard it again. As if she was impatient with him, her feet were tapping against the magazine, which was lodged between a cushion and one of the arms of the sofa. Reaching behind him, Shurnas pulled the magazine free and threw it on the floor. In a while, with Jackie asleep under him, he reached for the light.

Toward morning they both rose and made the sofa up into a bed. Jackie went back to sleep instantly, but Shurnas, feeling the apartment as too warm now that the sun was coming up, decided to put on the air conditioner. Because the room was small it got cold very quickly. Close to sleep himself by now, Shurnas could not make himself rise to turn off the air conditioner. He pulled the sheet up over his face and fitted himself against Jackie whose back was to him.

With the sheet covering his eyes he was overcome by the sensation that the person beside him was not Jackie. He tried to identify the features that were distinctly hers, but he couldn't come up with any—not even her smell, which he remembered as being extraordinarily clean and cool, but now, after having been blended all night with his own smell and those confined in the sofa, seemed quite musky. He closed his eyes and for a long while studied the picture of her body that he had carried in his mind all the past year, concentrating in particular on her hips, thighs and legs. Every now and then he had to open his eyes to reassure himself that she was really beside him, that someone was beside him anyway; in the grayness he could make out only a dim shape under the sheet. He resorted to thinking about the woman in the sauna, in the hope that the contrast between the memory he had of her and those he had of Jackie would produce some detail he could fix on. The matted pubic hair was no help. Jackie's pubic hair on

18

the afternoons she had grudgingly let him remove her bathing suit last summer, after swimming, had also been matted. Her vagina, he remembered, had tasted strongly of chlorine, but what woman's wouldn't after swimming in a pool. Suddenly, thinking of going down on her, he recalled how tense she would get whenever he tried to give her a rim job. There was a smooth flange of skin between her vagina and anus that made her very self-conscious. To the touch it felt like a hemorrhoid, but she claimed it had occurred in the process of giving birth to an illegitimate child. In addition she had stretch marks on her stomach, but many women who'd been pregnant had those whereas the flange of skin, to Shurnas's experience, was totally unique. It was no use: he slipped his hand between her legs and began probing for the flange when he could no longer stand not knowing if it was really Jackie beside him. He felt her roll away from him and watched her wrap herself in the sheet.

Shurnas grew depressed. The feeling of isolation, now that she had separated herself from him, was even worse than the feeling she was a total stranger while they lay against each other. He tried to find another word for her behavior besides rejection. "Maybe it's just that you don't know how to allow other people space," he told himself. He remembered then that this had been one woman's explanation—even her exact words—for why she felt so smothered around him. Realizing that ever since Jackie had taken all of the sheet for herself he had been lying uncovered, he also realized that curiously he did not feel cold, although the flow of air from the air conditioner was so strong that, in the narrow beam of sunlight from the window that fell across his legs, he saw it stirring the hair on them. Somehow it seemed that he could continue not feeling the air conditioner if he did not have to see the effects of it.

Jackie was awake when he returned to bed after drawing the

blind. Even though the room was surprisingly dark, he could see her eyes—perhaps because they stood out more now that the rest of her was so tanned.

"What time is it?" she said.

Feeling her question implied a criticism of him, Shurnas didn't reply for a moment. Then, afraid she was going to repeat it, he said, "Still early."

Would he mind if she didn't get up to see him out when he left? She was really feeling pitted out.

"Pitted out?"

Certain that he had never heard anyone except Jackie use that expression and glad that he now had incontrovertible evidence of her presence here, he began rubbing her back. When she pushed his hand away, he felt a chill that came over him not from within himself but from the air conditioner, the hum of which was rapidly becoming an intrusion anyway. He turned it off and grew aware that it wasn't the sound he had been hearing after all. Rather, there seemed to be a faint singing in his ears.

The air in the room felt, within seconds after the air conditioner was off, as if each breath he drew was going to be more impossible than the one before it. Watching his chest muscles expand and contract, Shurnas could not accept that Jackie needed the sheet around her when he was perspiring. It amazed him that he could still be shaking as if chilled when his throat and mouth felt parched. Almost absently, he began to rub Jackie's back again but stopped when she said, "Give me a break."

Shurnas didn't want an argument. He would have said something conciliatory to her, but she'd pulled the pillow over her head. In a while she raised it with both hands and looked as if she was about to fling it at something. "You have to leave," she said. "Really. You have to get out of here." Shurnas, who was having trouble with his ears again, silently watched her clutch the pillow against her breasts and bury her face in it.

When she threw the sheet off herself saying, "What happened to the air conditioner—did you break it?" Shurnas finally had to ask her about her tan. From her silence, he understood she had been sunbathing nude with a man. "Well, it looks good on you," he said. While he was studying her, he saw that her body, in the dark room, actually looked quite pale. Later he noticed that, for all her complaining about the air conditioner not being on, she wasn't perspiring whereas his side of the mattress was soaked and he was having, every few moments or so, to mop his forehead with his hand. Similarly, her breathing had a regular rhythm to it and his own sounded a little like it did after he'd just finished a long rally on the tennis court. It disturbed him that his body, which was in perfect shape except for the bruise on his knee, was showing much more strain than hers, especially since, other than lying in the sun, she did nothing to take care of herself. "Women have an edge," he told himself, although he did not think he really believed that. But it was definite that every glimpse of her body and its lack of movement prevented him from feeling at home any longer in his own body; and he was jealous that she, a woman, seemed able to exist so independent of her surroundings.

In a while he noticed that his body was being compelled to do things to counteract the stillness of hers—scratch his leg audibly with his fingernails, sigh heavily, shift his weight on the mattress so that the springs creaked. He even thought of turning on the air conditioner again so he could hear its hum.

But then he noticed that, although he hadn't once taken his eyes off Jackie, she had somehow managed to move without his seeing it. The pillow, instead of being clutched to her breasts, was covering her head again. He wanted to touch her but didn't dare for fear it would provoke her to repeat that he had to leave. Restless, he began walking around the room;

21

from time to time he glanced at her, but if she moved again he missed it. Running out of things to do, he sat down on the mattress and asked if she was asleep. When she didn't answer he resented it, but he resented the sound of his own voice more. Every word he uttered at this stage only increased the distance he felt between them, and it angered him that he was forced to think in those terms. *Distance. Space.*

Without intending anything more than to relieve some of his restlessness, he pulled the pillow away from Jackie with the idea of squeezing it between his hands. At first, when she grabbed it back from him, he thought he was struggling with her for possession of it, but then, gradually, he realized he was pressing it against her face. He heard something hit the floor in the apartment above hers. Too nervous to tell if it was another coin, he noticed Jackie's hands were no longer on the pillow. They were flailing about, and one of them, the right one, was slapping his arms. Then she suddenly stopped trying to fight him and he heard a muffled noise. It sounded as if she was trying to tell him something. But when he removed the pillow from her face she just lay there with wide-open eyes.

The conclusion was so unavoidable that he began chilling all over his body again. Strangely, when he turned on the air conditioner, the chill went away, replaced for a moment by a fresh burst of perspiration. Then that stopped too, and he began hearing the sound of the air conditioner. He refused to listen. Right away he grew aware of his breathing. As he was dressing he inspected himself. The bruise on his knee seemed smaller today. Which meant he must have gotten a decent night's sleep here after all.

It took him awhile to find Jackie's purse; then her door key wasn't in it. And one or the other of them had left some mud on the carpet. Remembering the running shoes he had seen under the sofa, he understood she must have hauled it in on the bottoms of them. The room had grown quite cold again.

22

"Where's the key?" he heard himself say. Turning off the air conditioner make him think of turning on the light. Once he had, he realized there was nothing he really wanted to see. The key wasn't going to make any difference; her door locked automatically anyway, and to double-lock it, from outside, would be a giveaway that someone else had been there.

He went into the bathroom. When he pulled back the shower curtain, he saw that the tub was filled with stockings and underwear that had been left to soak. Faced with that kind of domesticity, he could hardly take a shower badly as he wanted one. He could barely wash his hands and face, being careful not to catch himself looking at himself in the mirror over the sink. Finished, he dried himself with a towel, which he then used to wipe off everything he had come in contact with here, pausing now and then to scrape a handful of mud off the carpet and toss it on the bed so that the entire place would have a more uniform look.

The magazine he nearly stepped on in leaving was the same one he had been reading last night. Thinking he would finish the story about the apartment hunters on the subway, he put it under his arm. As he stepped out of the building, he held the magazine over his face like a visor, not only because it hid him from view but also because it would seem natural to anyone watching that someone coming outside for the first time that day was using it as a shield against the sun. But then he saw it was dark. His watch, which had said eleven o'clock when he looked at it a few moments ago, now said five after eleven. At night? As always, when things were later than he had anticipated, he felt panic. Throwing the magazine into a trash basket, he went into the bar on the corner of Jackie's block and used the same pay phone he had used last night to call the same woman. He was relieved when she was not home: it would have been a deliberate recapturing of the past if she had been.

He was going to have a drink at the bar before he left but

became afraid that as a stranger there he would attract attention. As he started toward the subway station, he remembered another bar not far from Jackie's neighborhood where he was better known. Once there, he decided he didn't really want a drink after all. While waiting for the pay phone to be free, he ordered a sandwich and ate it standing up at the bar. The number he dialed was busy. He counted to a hundred, then dialed it again. The woman who answered made him repeat his name three times before acknowledging that she knew who was calling, but she immediately invited him to "come up for a nightcap" when he told her he was in the neighborhood. The fact was she lived clear across town, on York Avenue, and even a cab ride to her place would take half an hour; so, to explain away the time lag, Shurnas told her he first had to check in with his answering service and follow up on any calls for lessons that had come in.

He got to York Avenue around midnight and received a nod, when he entered her building, from the doorman who appeared to recognize him although it had been a good while since he had last been there. Upon leaving the elevator, he stood for nearly a minute getting his bearings before he remembered which direction to take down the hallway. When he knocked on her door, he heard her tell him to come in. "It's open." It disturbed him that she had so casually left her door unlocked even though she knew he'd be along shortly. As he closed the door behind him, listening to the lock catch, it occurred to him that she hadn't even bothered to make sure he was the person who'd knocked before inviting him in. He meant to tell her that the sense of security the doorman provided was false—true, the man might have a good memory for faces that belonged in the building, but no one was infallible.

The bed was separated from the rest of her studio apartment by a plasterboard partition. Hearing a TV set playing behind the partition, Shurnas understood, after glancing around the apartment and not seeing her, that she was waiting for him in bed. He would have liked a shower before joining her but didn't know how to suggest this.

When he peeked around the side of the partition, she said, "I was just thinking about you today." She was sitting up in bed. Because all the lights were out, Shurnas couldn't tell if the thing she was wearing was a shortie nightgown or just a shirt. On the table beside the bed were a bottle of wine and plate of cheese and crackers. On a larger table at the foot of the bed were a portable TV set and an electric fan. The fan was causing the picture on the TV set to waver a bit. Shurnas, thinking that he was going to have to start eating better, picked up a cracker and sat beside her on the bed. Despite the noises made by the TV set and the fan, he heard her "umm-m" sound as he reached for her.

CHAPTER TWO

When he woke up in the morning, the TV set and the fan were still going. "It's supposed to be another scorcher," the woman said. She was sitting on the edge of the bed watching *Good Morning America*. As soon as his eyes were open, Shurnas checked the bruise on his knee. Upon seeing that the discoloration seemed lighter today than yesterday, he thought: "At least it isn't turning into phlebitis." The woman got up and went to do some things on the other side of the partition. Shurnas, beginning to dress, realized this was going to be the third day in a row he had worn the same clothes. Did he want to take a shower? he heard her call.

A few minutes later, drying himself in the tub while she put on her makeup in front of the mirror, he was interested in how drastically her reflection changed with each new color she applied to her face. "Putting on the war paint," he murmured, but no meaningful conversation occurred between them until they sat down to breakfast—nothing but black coffee since she was on a diet. He asked about her job, she asked about his; she told him what she had been doing of late and he filled her in on some of the more recent details of his own life.

"See *Interiors* yet?"

"No, have you?"

"I took a half share in a house on Fire Island."

"The club's been keeping me really busy; I haven't had any real time off since April." He was on the verge of telling her about the tournament match but changed his mind when he realized that she didn't know enough about tennis to understand the intricacies of the story.

"Sometime you're going to have to take me to Central Park and give me a few lessons," she said. "I even bought a parks department permit this year so I could play, but there's never anyone to play with."

He told her there was lots of time yet, the summer wasn't even half over.

Then she asked him if he wanted to stay in her apartment for a few days; she had to go to Chicago for a buyers' convention and wouldn't mind having someone around to look after the place. "There've been quite a few robberies lately in this building," she said. "People on vacation." Now was the opportunity to mention the paradox between her concern over being robbed and the careless manner in which she had awaited his arrival last night, but suddenly Shurnas seemed to recall that he had made an arrangement with her in the past that was similar to the one she was now suggesting. "Did I leave some clothes here?" he said.

By the time the woman had packed her suitcase—she was flying to Chicago right after work that afternoon—and left, it was nearly time for Shurnas to be at the club. Having found a shirt and a pair of pants to fit him on a hanger in her closet, he dropped the clothes he had worn since Saturday at a cleaners across the street from her building. Because he was running a little late, he didn't look at the *News* he'd bought at a stand on East 86th Street until he reached the subway platform. There he saw the headline story was about another woman jogger— "the fourth since last fall"—who had been found strangled in Central Park. Shurnas, who had never understood the running craze anyway, read only the first paragraph of the story before beginning to flip the pages for news of other ill-fated women. Then, taking a second glance at the front page, he realized his search was premature. For some reason, almost certainly because he, Shurnas, was a stranger to the neighborhood, he had been slipped an unsold copy of last night's early edition of the paper by the man behind the stand.

When the train came he peeled off the dozen or so pages of the paper that contained the sports news and threw the rest away. Then, feeling he'd acted too rashly—being on the Upper East Side he faced having to change trains at 59th Street and a fairly long ride to the club after that—he grabbed the bulk of the paper back from the trash barrel and jumped on the train just as the doors were closing. He would have enough to read now. In the event he ran out he could always do the crossword puzzle. As was typical after he'd had a day off from the club, he felt vaguely displaced. Within seconds after the train was underway, he was perspiring and his legs had turned to water. His was the sort of job, he decided, where you either had to take a lot of time off or none at all.

With a mimeographed schedule of that week's events at the club in his hand, he had gone straight to his locker upon arriving at the club and begun changing into a tennis outfit. On his way past the girl who ran the desk, he had avoided looking at her but was forced to make some greeting to her anyway when she said, "What's cooking, good-looking?" She was wearing a green tank top today without a bra. Even though he usually admired her breasts, often wondering what she did to make the nipples look so hard, this morning, walking with his eyes averted, he did not feel the slightest interest in her. Nevertheless he was thankful that she made everything around her desk seem more or less normal.

Since his day began with five hours of lessons in a row, Shurnas made sure he had enough change in the pocket of his shorts to get two Cokes on his break. Double his usual quota, but the quick sugar intake would be necessary if he was going to survive the heat out there. "Out there!" It was another of those catchy phrases women used on occasion to describe him.

"You think just because you're out there sexually, you're really out there." As he was changing the laces on his tennis shoes, the college player came in and asked him how his day off had been. "You're lucky you weren't working yesterday. I must've lost twenty pounds." For a moment, staring into his locker, Shurnas realized he was waiting for the college player to add "out there." It was already stifling in the small dressing room; the other pro had an electric fan, but it was locked in his locker and today was his day off.

The manager, who on most afternoons taught the Junior Development Program to make himself feel he was still a tennis pro, was sitting in his office in just a pair of gold running shorts. His torso gleamed with perspiration and there was a crushed soda can in his hand. Shurnas knew without being told that he was going to be stuck today with teaching the Junior Development Program on top of all his lessons. "I'll take it tomorrow," the manager said. "Besides, you're really good with kids." He handed Shurnas a circular for a tournament coming up later in the summer in New Jersey. Putting it in his pocket, Shurnas decided to quit. But the manager, glancing at his watch, had already picked up the phone with a comment that it was almost nine o'clock. Shurnas didn't recall leaving the manager's office, but when he glanced at his own watch the sunlight, reflecting off the crystal, was blinding. Someone had handed him a basket of balls. Looking up from his watch, he saw a woman in a dazzling white tennis dress standing in front of him. "When am I going to get to practice my net game?" she asked. Her nose was badly sunburned. Shurnas wanted to tell her to put some zinc oxide on it but felt sure she would rather he hadn't noticed.

He hit balls for a while to the woman at the net, though of course she missed most of them. Finally she smacked a volley that landed squarely on the baseline. "Yes!" Shurnas said. "That's the shot. You've got it." He moved her back from the net and worked for the rest of the hour on her crosscourt forehand, her best shot and the only one she really cared about.

Around noon one of the male club members came in for a playing lesson. The man worked on Wall Street but took a cab all the way to Queens on his lunch hour just so he could play a set or two with Shurnas. During the warmup before they started Shurnas took it easy. The sun was beating directly down on the court; the soles of his feet even though they were protected by two pairs of socks, felt as if they were scalded. When play started he hit the ball hard, but refrained from running all out for shots. Still he beat the man 6-0, 6-1.

At the end of the hour, shaking hands with Shurnas, the man said, "I don't know how you do it. You always look like you're losing, but you never do." When Shurnas looked down after the man's hand had been extracted from his, there was a ten-dollar tip in his palm. He had enough time before his next lesson to grab a bite to eat but didn't because his stomach felt too skittish. Besides, he was looking forward to a good dinner later on.

Less than half the kids who were registered for the Junior Development Program showed up; Shurnas supposed most of them had gone to the beach for the day. Of the kids who were there, only one of them—the daughter of a woman everyone at the club knew the manager was sleeping with—had any real promise. Envisioning the girl, under his coaching, as a future Billie Jean King, Shurnas wished it had been in the cards for him to have children. While showing her the grip for two-handed backhand, he found himself smelling her hair as he looked down over her shoulder at her fingers on the racket handle. It had an herbal fragrance that he had learned to associate with a particular brand of shampoo. "For radiant clean hair." The girl was the right age to have been his daughter if she had not been so naturally blond; no one Shurnas ever been seriously associated with had anything but dark hair.

At the end of the day, having no good reason for refusing, Shurnas accepted a ride to Manhattan with the manager. He remembered to take his address book out of his locker but left a half-finished can of Coke in the shower. As they drove along Queens Boulevard, the car's engine made a pinging sound that the manager said to ignore because he was thinking of junking the car anyway. In fact Shurnas could have it for $100. Shurnas, who cared little about cars but felt left out because he didn't have one, immediately grew tense with thoughts of the lines he would have to stand on to transfer the title, buy license plates, etc. His silence had an unexpected effect, in that the manager went on to say that Shurnas could have the car for nothing if he waited a few days until the new Toyota the manager had ordered came in. "They offered me $200 on a trade-in, but for that kind of money I'd rather see it go to a friend."

Confused whether the panic he felt was caused by the manager having so off-handedly called him a friend or by his fear of committing himself to anything too complicated, Shurnas said, "Let me sleep on the idea."

He noticed when they were crossing the Queensboro Bridge that the manager was playing with the dials on the radio as if to prove they were all in working order. Music blared, so loud at times that people in neighboring cars glared at them. Still, in all, Shurnas considered the radio on the plus side in weighing the factors that were going into his decision on the car. Then he noticed that the manager, not having been told any different, was taking him to his place on West 19th Street. He got out on the corner, waited for the manager's car to disappear around the next corner, then walked to the subway entrance on 18th Street. He took a "1" train to Times Square, changed to a shuttle and rode it to Grand Central. There he caught a number "4" train to 86th Street. The whole trip, including the drive to Manhattan, took considerably longer than if he had taken a train home from the club in the first place; and when he stopped at the stand where he had bought a paper that morning, he was too late to get a copy of the *Post*. All during the ride uptown he had planned on saying something about having been "mistakenly" given the wrong edition of the *News*, but the man who told him the *Post* was all sold out was not the same one who had been behind the stand that morning.

The trash baskets he looked into as he walked along 86th Street had numerous copies of the morning papers but none of the *Post*. Shurnas did not see this as necessarily diabolical: the odds were still in his favor that he would find a *Post* when he went out later in the evening. As he entered the woman's building on York Avenue, the doorman did not meet his eyes, but there was nothing judgmental about it: the haste with which the man opened the door for him was no more or less than that accorded regular tenants. In the elevator, going up, Shurnas was alone.

Between opening the window and turning on the fan, he got the woman's apartment fairly cool in a hurry. After a while—the apartment faced east so he couldn't see how close the sun was to setting—he gave up trying to get anyone on the phone and began looking around for something to eat. "Soul food," he said when he opened the refrigerator and saw little but containers of yogurt. In the cupboard he found a half-empty box of spaghetti and a can of red tomato sauce; though he would have preferred another color, he could see where it didn't make that much difference. As soon as the pot of water on the stove came to a boil, the phone rang. Thinking it was the stewardess from American Airlines for whom he had left a message at the American flight desk when he learned she was booked to fly in from San Francisco that evening, he turned the stove off, contemplating the steak and ale they would have in her room. But it was the woman calling from Chicago to tell him her plane had arrived safely. Shurnas had forgotten the circumstances under which he was staying in her apartment. He asked her whether she had to pay for the call, but she'd begun talking about the weather. "It's even worse here than it is in New York," she said. Shurnas, not sure what she meant by worse, did not inquire.

When she hung up—"See you Wednesday. Change the sheets if you do anything naughty."—he finally had a chance to feel at home. While he ate his spaghetti, he glanced through his address book. He soon noticed that many more of the women's names he'd crossed out began with D than the law of averages allowed. Clearly now, he understood that the stewardess, whose name was Deirdre, wasn't going to return his call. "Scratch one pair of wings," he said, mentally drawing a line through her name because in looking around he didn't see a pen. As he continued eating red splotches of tomato sauce began to appear on the pages of his address book.

Later he took the phone off the hook. Then he decided to call his answering service and had to wait for the dial tone to be restored. The girl's voice on the other end had three messages for him that had left phone numbers and one that had not. This last message had come from Shurnas's ex-wife whose name, although it did not begin with D, had been crossed out in his address book several months ago when he realized her phone number was so indelibly imprinted on his mind that it wasn't necessary to have it in writing.

It irritated Shurnas, when he called his ex-wife, to get a recording saying she wasn't taking any calls until after the opening of her new painting exhibition. About to hang up, he heard her voice rattle off the address of an art gallery on Prince Street. "And don't worry—there'll be plenty of booze." Her voice laughed rather wildly. Shurnas supposed she had made the recording while high on some drug. He had to dial her number a second time so he could get the recording to repeat the address of the gallery and the time of the opening. It was tomorrow afternoon at five o'clock. Putting himself in her mind, he understood that the call to his answering service had been her way of making sure he found out about the opening, and he wondered why she hadn't sent him a written invitation. Then it occurred to him that she must know he hadn't been home in a while to pick up his mail. This, to Shurnas's thinking, seemed entirely plausible. Among their problems while they were married hadn't been a lack of communication.

The TV set was even wavier tonight than it had been last night. Since it was a Monday there should have been a baseball game on ABC, but Shurnas, fooling with the color knob, saw they were going to show a movie instead. Evidently the game had been postponed. That seemed to mean it could still rain other places even if it never rained here. If it had been a neighborhood he liked better, he probably would have tried to find a bar. The Upper East Side, though, wasn't a place you could call home. He started to make the bed, which the woman hadn't had time to do before leaving that morning, but then he realized he was going to lie down for a while.

Without undressing, he played with the fan until he got the blades aimed at an angle that blew air directly into his face as he lay on his back. When he awakened sometime after midnight he had a stiff neck. Everything else about him felt sticky with perspiration. Still he did not undress because he thought he was going out at any moment to look for a *Post*. In a while it struck him that if he had awakened earlier he could have watched the news on TV and gotten the same information. Shurnas had trouble imagining what that information would be. Lying there, he began to see himself getting up and being careful to lock the door of the woman's apartment behind him. Out on the street, in a trash basket, a copy of the *Post* stuck straight up in the air like a sail; he was walking toward it when his head turned on the pillow so that it was out of range of the fan.

In the morning, after making sure this time that he actually had the late edition in his hand before he paid his twenty cents, he read the *News* from cover to cover while riding the subway to the club. But he learned little other than that the police had unearthed a pattern to the murders of the women joggers; all of them had been wearing blue running shoes when their bodies were found. "It might mean nothing," someone identified only as a police spokesman had said. "Or it might mean everything." The Yankees meanwhile had won on a homer by Reggie Jackson. Shurnas, who was not accustomed to reading so intently, noticed he had a stiff neck again by the end of the ride. Luckily he didn't have an early lesson scheduled that morning, so he could sit awhile in the sauna. Once there, he stopped the head rotations he had been doing to loosen his neck when he saw that under the initials R.T. someone had scrawled "M.R.S.". Of course others in the world had the same initials he did, including the manager of the club for one, but there could nevertheless be messages here. He recalled that the college player was off today, so there was no one he could ask if the sauna woman's name was Rose.

By ten o'clock all of Shurnas's lessons that day had called the club to cancel; nobody was on any of the courts; the temperature was already close to 100 degrees. When over coffee in the women's dressing room—which for no accountable reason was cooler than the men's—the manager brought up the subject of his car again, Shurnas offered to play the manager a match that very minute for its ownership. "I'll put up $100 and you put up the keys." Shurnas assumed the manager knew he was joking and was just playing along with it when he said, "No, what you have to do is put up a dollar for every degree it is on the court when we start play." But then the manager got up and left the room. When he returned he said, "I just called the weather—it's ninety-eight in the shade."

Shurnas, smiling, suggested they play nude like the Greek

Olympians and felt a little nervous upon hearing the manager say, very earnestly, that he supposed, since none of the club members were around, they could relax the rule about not playing without shirts. Around then, although the way the manager was talking could still have been a put-on, Shurnas began to experience the same lightheadedness that he always did before an important match. Already sensing he would need witnesses, he regretted that the girl who ran the desk had called in sick today and that the other pro was in Manhattan buying trophies for the club mixed doubles tournament that weekend.

"Your choice," the manager told him. "Two out of three sets or one eight-game pro set for all the marbles." Shurnas, who hadn't played the manager since losing purposely to him the day he was hired, was gradually realizing that very few people nowadays shared his sense of humor. He noticed that the manager had changed from running shorts to tennis shorts while out of the room. As he threw his coffee cup into the waste basket, he saw it was going to land on top of a tampax wrapper. "I play for the crowd." Not long ago, on a TV interview after the Wimbledon finals, he had heard last year's women's singles champion say that.

Neither Shurnas nor the manager spoke during the warm-up. Before serving to begin the match, Shurnas, having opted to play two out of three sets in the belief that the manager, being a much older man, would wilt in the heat, remembered the bruise on his knee. When he looked down it appeared to be gone, although it was true that, with the sun in his eyes, the flesh on his leg was not its normal color but that of chalk. He noticed the manager's face was a similar color, but the sun wasn't responsible for that. Because the street outside the club had a lot of traffic, the manager was wearing a surgical mask.

Shurnas tossed the ball in the air, swung his racket into it and served an ace: the manager didn't even blink until the ball was past him. The rest of the set was just as easy. Shurnas, who knew his greatest enemy was overconfidence, absorbed himself in thoughts of where he would go for a new job after he was fired for beating the manager. Between sets he wiped the perspiration off the handle of his racket with a towel. When had he ever felt more invincible? He started onto the court again and saw that all the lines on it were shimmering. Before putting the towel down he vomitted a mouthful of a brown substance into it that tasted like burned coffee. "I warned you to start eating right," he told himself. The manager, standing in the distance with both feet together like a soldier at attention, signaled he was ready to resume play by holding up a ball. It had been green when the match started but now, perhaps because it was soaked with perspiration from having been held so often in sweaty hands, Shurnas saw that it looked almost black. The strings of his racket, which he was gazing through in the hope their pattern would make the lines on the court stop moving, looked orange. Disgusted with seeing so many things in terms of their color, Shurnas flung the towel aside. As he walked toward the baseline to receive the manager's serve, he saw a black trail of spots forming on the court, though it was indefinite whether they were drops of perspiration falling from his body or some deception, now of all things, involving his eyes.

The manager began trying to copy Shurnas's style of play. Every time Shurnas hit a hard shot, the manager hit a hard one back. If Shurnas threw up a high lob, he got a lob in return. At first Shurnas, still not seeing things in their proper color, didn't detect the strategy in this, but eventually he realized the manager was making it seem as if he was shadow-boxing with himself. So he wouldn't be swallowed up by sameness, he narrowed his eyes and told himself, "Don't let it go to your head." But the expression made no sense to him although he heard others use it all the time. The word head combined with the phrase go to? With a possessive pronoun in front of it head became a noun representing your emotional equilibrium. Put the article "the" in front of it, however, and it changed to a slang term for bathroom. Substitute "you" or "me" for the and the phrase took on a sexual meaning. But no. You couldn't say go to; it had to be "give" you or "give" me. Shurnas grew dizzy. The lightness he had felt before the start of the match returned to his head. And there it was again. After his shock at having been forced to use the word in a whole new phrase, he couldn't concentrate on anything else. He crouched—in wait for the manager to serve. Because the manager had just finished serving, he in turn was waiting for Shurnas to pick up the ball, which lay behind him.

While Shurnas was serving a few minutes later with the set tied four-all, he hit an ace only to hear the manager claim he hadn't been ready and demand that he serve over. With no strength left to waste arguing, Shurnas simply smiled tightly at the manager to show his opinion of this ploy. Then he felt he was letting the heat deprive him of his natural competitive instincts, and he started toward the net as if to debate the issue further. Now that he was in closer quarters, he noticed a dark stain on the crotch of the manager's tennis shorts. In line with all the other tricks the sun had been playing on his eyes, Shurnas supposed the stain was an illusion. Hoping if he didn't comment on it the manager wouldn't ask him what he was staring at, he turned and went back to the baseline.

On his next serve there had been, despite all his guarding against it, an incident. The manager had hit the return into the net, then raised his hand after a long hesitation to call the serve no good. After several more moments had passed, during which Shurnas stared at the blur the sun had made out of his racket, the manager walked slowly up to the net and picked up the ball so as to clear the court. Shurnas saw him then walk back to the baseline with the ball in his hand. He took his eyes away from the manager to check the alignment of his feet before cocking his racket to deliver his second serve.

When Shurnas raised his eyes again, he saw that he had turned away to adjust the surgical mask which had slipped off his nose in bending to pick up the ball. The air over the courts—which had never impressed Shurnas as being all that bad—suddenly seemed stifling. Gasping, he shouted something when he couldn't stand it any longer. In the stillness his shout sounded hollow to his own ears, like an echo.

Upon realizing that the manager was finally in position again to receive his serve, Shurnas raised two fingers questioningly, morally certain that because of his opponent's delaying tactics he should be granted two serves, but the other man raised one finger and shook his head. "Play one," he barked from behind the surgical mask.

Whereas his own shout had only amplified the stillness, the manager's voice destroyed it. Startled at the number of other sounds he suddenly began hearing—birds, a phone ringing in an apartment building across the street from the club, way off in the distance the clanging of an elevated train—he dropped his racket. It made yet another sound he had to contend with as it landed on the court. The manager continued to stand on the baseline but not as if he was still waiting to receive Shurnas's serve or even as if he had any more interest in Shurnas's serve. Shurnas saw him tug at the crotch of his shorts. Thinking of the dark stain he had seen there a few minutes ago, Shurnas bent to pick up his racket—but then he noticed that he must have already performed this movement because the racket was back in his hand again. In a moment, concentrating, he realized it was in his left hand. With the ball he had been going to serve with in his right hand, he walked off the court. On his way out the gate which separated the courts from the clubhouse, he ran into the other pro who was carrying a large silver trophy under each arm. Out of professional jealousy he seldom acknowledged Shurnas, but now, blocking Shurnas's path to the clubhouse, he seemed to wink.

No more than a minute later, while sitting in front of his locker in the small room behind the pro shop, Shurnas realized he was no longer alone. Without looking around, he waited for the manager's hand to be put on his shoulder. When he felt it there, he understood he had been fired. Gradually he realized he was waiting for something more to happen. Logically, since he'd been fired, it followed that he'd won the match and therefore the ownership of the manager's car. "Where's the key?" he said. The sound of his own voice chilled him.

The manager, who made the usual remarks about giving Shurnas a good recommendation, etc., looked elsewhere as he spoke as though there were other things in the room he had to keep an eye on. "You're a good teacher," he said. "Especially with kids." The word kids naturally caused Shurnas to wince. On the floor, partially hidden under the locker beside his, he saw a red headband of the type the college player sometimes wore. The manager put his hands in the pockets of his shorts. His eyes also appeared to notice the headband. Which one of us will break down and pick it up? Shurnas wondered. It angered him that he couldn't make others understand that everything didn't have to be a contest just because it felt like one. To prove he wasn't feeling any pressure he bent to pick up the headband, then stopped himself when he realized the act of picking it up would demonstrate his participation in the contest.

Looking around the room, he began seeing other items that could be made into a contest if he had that kind of mind. Under his own locker there was an empty Coke can. Near the wall, in plain sight of both Shurnas and the manager, a bench had been overturned. Shurnas attempted to rise, but the manager was watching him. Sitting down again, he waited for the other man to leave the room. At last, rid of the crowded feeling, he began to perspire freely. The headband was actually,

40

now that he had an opportunity to look at it alone, the one he had worn in the match today.

The manager had come back and was standing in the doorway. In his hand was a piece of paper, but when he went to hand it to Shurnas, who thought it was his final pay check, one or the other of them didn't reach far enough. Shurnas watched the paper fall to the floor. Was this the beginning of another contest? "Look on the back, you'll see I claimed I gave it to you as a gift," the manager said. "That's so you don't have to pay sales tax." When the manager had gone, Shurnas leaned forward and discovered the paper was the title to the manager's car. Later, as he was cleaning out his locker, the other pro stopped by to shake hands and say, "Murray said to remind you to make sure and get the car signed over into your own name at Motor Vehicles this afternoon." When Shurnas nodded the man, as if it was an afterthought, mentioned a club in the Bronx where he knew of an opening for a teaching pro. Shurnas, unable to stand all these amenities, went back to cleaning out his locker.

The manager's car was parked behind the club, but when Shurnas went to look, the key was not in the ignition. So as not to seem foolish, he checked his pockets before returning to the club. Once inside, he remembered that the other pro had given him an envelope which he had been too distracted by the handshaking ritual to open. The envelope was still in his locker, along with some towels he had meant to leave behind. Removing the envelope from the locker made the towels too conspicuous, as though they could be interpreted as a statement on his part. He threw them into his equipment bag and ran out of the club.

Immediately upon getting into the manager's car he was glad he had the towels because he needed something to put down on the seat cover, which was so hot from the sun that his fingers stuck to the plastic as if they had melted into it. The key he found in the envelope was also quite warm, but so for that matter was the key to the woman's apartment when he linked the car key to the ring on it. He recalled suddenly that the key to his own apartment was in the pocket of the pants he had taken to the cleaners yesterday. It was enough to make him swear at himself, especially since his ex-wife, who was scarcely a model of organization herself, had the only duplicate of his key.

When he had driven a few blocks he passed a public swimming pool, but there were so many cars in the vicinity of it that he had to circle for several minutes before he found a parking place. There was a phone booth across the street. Shurnas tried to call a woman he knew who was a teacher and had her summers free, but she wasn't home. Undoubtedly, on a day like this, she had long since departed for the beach. It struck him then that the beach made more sense than a swimming pool. Pools had a way of making him faintly despondent, mostly because he couldn't help but notice while lying beside them that even though they were roughly the same dimensions as a tennis court, all the water in them played havoc with the lines on their bottoms. "Life's distorted enough as it is," he thought, meanwhile looking at his watch. The rest of the day, although he could think of no reason why it wasn't his to do with as he wished, was making him feel rushed.

He got on the Brooklyn-Queens Expressway, passed the Williamsburg, Manhattan and Brooklyn Bridges, and headed south for a while. Eventually he found himself following a long stream of cars across a toll bridge that led to the Rockaways. On the other side of the bridge a policeman was directing traffic into two lanes, one of which went nowhere in particular and the other of which led to a public beach called Riis Park. Shurnas, seeing both advantages and disadvantages in each lane, waited for an impulse to take him over. None did. In the end, to get out of feeling oppressed by all the cars around

42

him, he went to Riis Park, where he immediately faced another kind of oppression when he discovered there were lines to get into the parking lot.

As soon as he got on the beach he felt that he should have gone to a pool. The ocean still looked as murky as ever, and the same women still seemed to be lying on their stomachs with the bra straps of their bathing suits trailing loose in the sand. Then, walking past a section of the beach where there were fewer kids, Shurnas felt as if there had been at least one change. Several people, to his astonishment, were sunbathing nude. Farther along he saw a lone girl lying near some rocks and very obviously desiring the seclusion they brought her. She was spreading suntan lotion on her thighs with one hand as her other hand slowly peeled off a pair of cutoff jeans. When the cutoffs were removed she was totally nude except for some bracelets on her wrists. To Shurnas's eye her body was a little too meager to really be called attractive, but he liked the gypsy appearance the bracelets gave her. Although he had no intention of disturbing the girl, he put his towel down a few feet away from her and sat on it.

Somebody screamed. When Shurnas looked up, expecting to find out that the scream had been a warning the police were coming, a woman was rolling in the surf right in front of him. The woman screamed again, evidently to show being knocked about by waves was her idea of a good time. Shurnas thought things over and decided that while he could probably take his clothes off here without being arrested, it would serve no useful purpose. "Like a hard-on in a porn shop," he thought. He leaned back on his elbows so he could feel the sun on his face. In a while he removed his shirt and rolled his pants up to his knees. He was wearing tennis shorts under the pants but could see, if he stripped down to them, that the girl, who had moved even closer to the rocks, might begin to feel an intrusion.

Later he took off all his clothes because the girl, having

43

fallen asleep on her stomach, could not be possibly watching him.

The beach had become quite crowded; not too many people were nude, but among those who were was a fat man with an erection. Shurnas was sitting so close to him that he could easily have been convinced that he felt an intrusion of sorts himself. As he moved his towel away from the man, he was aware that he was at the same time moving closer to the girl. When she awakened he smiled at her and told her she had the right idea. All he meant was that it was cooler by the rocks, but immediately afraid she would find another meaning in his remark, he added that he was surprised nude sunbathing had become legal on a city beach. The girl, explaining that Riis Park was now federally owned, shifted her towel so that her back was to him. Assuming that was the end of the conversation between them, Shurnas thought he would swim for a while. Besides, he had to find someplace to urinate. But when he came out of the water the girl said, "Hey—better put something on next time you go in." She began to tell Shurnas that the relaxation of the laws on sunbathing did not extend to swimming, and Shurnas saw there were opportunities, as in any paradoxical situation, to make this into a full-fledged discussion. In time, although the girl continued to lie with her back to him, they got to know quite a bit about each other's attitudes.

Between talking and listening, Shurnas had no desire to go in the water again. True, his skin had begun feeling hot to the touch, as had the plastic seat cover in the manager's car—but no sooner did this analogy occur to him than he realized he had to stop thinking in those terms because the car was now his. "For better or for worse," he thought, then wished he'd chosen another expression because a car, as it was, could too easily start feeling like a marriage. In a while he mentioned to the girl that he was driving into Manhattan if she wanted a lift. "I took a bus out here," she said. Shurnas stared at the ocean, trying to decide what this information had told him. "Can you drop me someplace around Flatbush and Nostrand?" she went on. "I can get a train home from there." When they had dressed and were walking through the underpass to the parking lot, the girl turned to him and kissed him violently. As she pulled her mouth away from his, he felt her hand touch him—so lingeringly that it couldn't have been an accident. With all this intimacy, Shurnas felt that any further conversation between them would be a crime.

The traffic on the way back was heavy. Because it was frequently necessary to shift gears, Shurnas could use the hand that wasn't holding the steering wheel only intermittently to open his pants. Without taking his eyes off the road, he was aware of the girl's head going up and down in his lap. He drove cautiously. Through the windshield he watched the brake lights of the car ahead of him. Each time they came on he relaxed his foot on the gas pedal and reached for the gearshift. Eventually, at the end of a long line of cars waiting for the light at the intersection of Avenue U, he came. When he looked down he noticed that the girl had one of the towels he'd spread over the seat cover pressed to her mouth. It discouraged him that a connection, without his even trying, could be found between two disparate events. As if he'd known the towel would wind up having another use. According to his watch it was nearly five o'clock. So, among other things, there wasn't going to be time today to get to the Bureau of Motor Vehicles.

He noticed a newsstand near the subway entrance on Nostrand Avenue. As the girl started to get out of the car he handed her a quarter and asked her to buy a *Post* for him. "The late edition." His expectation was that she would simply hand the paper to him and then be on her way, but instead she climbed into the car again and started reading the headline story: NEW LEAD IN JOGGER SLAYINGS. "Man, am I glad I don't live in the city," the girl said. Since she'd told him she lived in Brooklyn, he glanced away in annoyance, not knowing how else to take people who viewed the city as consisting of nothing but Manhattan. What were the other boroughs—suburbs?

When the girl turned to one of the inside pages of the paper to read the continuation of the jogger story, Shurnas, looking over her shoulder, saw a short article that was headlined: SOCIAL WORKER A HEAT CASUALTY? He would have skipped ahead, believing the story held no interest to him, but then he remembered Jackie sometimes thought of herself as a social worker. Sitting there, his ears blocking out the girl's running commentary on the jogger story—"See, now they think it isn't the shoes that turn him on; it's the smell of perspiration!"—he allowed his mind slowly to yield to one word after another. That morning, when a young woman— "not identified by name, pending notification of next of kin"—had failed to report to work for the second day in a row, her supervisor, realizing it wasn't like her not to call if she was going to be absent, contacted a friend of hers who had a duplicate key to her apartment. Opening the door, the friend had been assailed by a "foul smell" and gone immediately to find the superintendent. The precinct had been called. "Like a tomb," one of the policemen, who had been among the first to enter the apartment, said. "We had to use gas masks, it was so bad."

"Mind if I take this along to read on the train?" the girl said. Looking up, Shurnas saw she had removed the center section of the paper and was getting out of the car with it. There was a faint line of perspiration between her eyebrows. Her mouth opened slightly as if she was going to say something else.

Or laugh?

Shurnas noticed she had tossed the rest of the paper in the back seat of the car on top of his tennis racket.

46

CHAPTER THREE

His ankle was hurting now. Shurnas didn't feel the match with the manager had taken a physical toll, so he must have twisted it on the beach. Driving was also a possible explanation, because his feet, unaccustomed to manipulating this pedal and that one, were beginning to feel a little weary. He crossed the Manhattan Bridge, stretching his legs between pedal respon-sibilities, and went west on Canal Street. Turning right on Centre Street, he had to hit the brake when a dog leaped out from between two parked cars, and his ankle ached sharply. When he got to the gallery where his ex-wife was having her opening, he was surprised to find so many empty parking places in front of it. Then, looking at a sign, he saw this was because they were illegal until six o'clock. His watch said twenty of. Twenty to? The correct phrasing, when you gave it some thought, should have been twenty before, and it irritated him that no one used it.

He parked across the street from the gallery and watched people going in and out of it for a while. His awareness of the car was so intense that his heart pounded. He was scared if he left it for even a minute it would be towed away. After a time a man on a bicycle came along. When the man began to chain the bicycle to a signpost in front of the gallery, Shurnas called to him out of the window of the car. Would they tow him away down here at twenty before the hour? The man didn't answer; Shurnas was certain this was because he refused to accept his usage of "before". He was about to say he meant twenty of the hour, but then he observed it was now closer to ten of.

When he looked up from his watch, the man was talking to a woman in front of the gallery. Now and then each of them threw a glance Shurnas's way but never at the same time, as if they were taking turns keeping him under observation. Shurnas found himself struggling against a feeling that they had teamed up to hold him there until the police came to tow him away. Then, thinking how unnecessarily he was worrying — the car, according to the law, wasn't even "officially" his yet — he rolled up the windows and started to get out. No sooner had he opened the door than the man called to him; something about being parked too close to the hydrant. Shurnas couldn't believe he had overlooked anything so obvious. Afraid that in another minute he would begin feeling totally defenseless, he quickly moved the car to another parking place where a mail truck hid him from the view of the man and the woman. By this time it was six minutes before — of — the hour. In a very short while now it would be possible to move around freely again.

His ankle was hurting now. Shurnas didn't feel the match with believe his watch was wrong when it said six, Shurnas felt it was safe to leave the car. Warily he entered the gallery, thankful that his ex wife had provided him with a legitimate motive for being there. For the moment she didn't seem to be around; at least he couldn't find her in the crowd, most of whom were gathered around a long table where a stubby woman in a low-cut dress was pouring wine into plastic cups. Glancing at the paintings on the walls, Shurnas noticed that all of them looked familiar. So it wasn't really an exhibition of his ex-wife's new art work after all. Although it was true that the paint on many of the canvasses still looked a little damp. He thought he recognized a portrait of himself, and it jolted him that he didn't remember posing for it. Although it was true it could have been reproduced from a photograph of him. He walked around, alternating between peering at the paintings and peering at the faces of the people looking at them.

Altogether it seemed to him that while the paintings were familiar, all of the people were complete strangers, as if in the time he and his ex-wife had been apart she had thrown over everyone in her past life. Since his own experience told him no one could ever really throw over anything, he would have believed he was in the wrong gallery if it had not been for the portrait of him.

He saw the man who had come to the gallery on a bicycle detach himself from the group around the long table, and he started toward him, feeling that as long as he was in the vicinity of the man, who had originally been encountered in the world outside the gallery and therefore was no longer a complete stranger, he would be all right. But the man walked away. Everyone else also seemed suddenly out of range. They were all so far away from Shurnas that even those whose voices reached him made gestures that had no relation to what their voices were saying. "Like when a movie track is out of synch," he thought, while trying not to overhear too much. For although he understood they were talking about his ex-wife's paintings, they could, the moment their gestures got in sequence with their words, turn on him. Too narcissistic. Too remote. Too self-indulgent. Too afraid of being accused of being subjective. The comments seemed—like the comments he was always listening to others make about him—to be uttered with such authority that there had to be a fundamental truth underlying their fundamental inconsistency.

The gallery had become so crowded that there was no place to stand without having to listen to someone. Shurnas retreated to a corner, put his eyes on a painting and kept them there. His clothes had a gritty feeling to them; he realized this was because they had sand in them from the beach. He shrugged his shoulders, jerked his arms, yanked his shirt collar away from his neck and shook it hard. At his feet, slowly, a thin layer of sand formed on the floor.

Gradually people in the gallery started leaving; others

49

trickled in the door and took their places. Shurnas had the impression that he was the one who was now out of range, as if, having gotten there ahead of the new arrivals, he had become a complete stranger to them rather than, as with the old crowd, they to him. Understandably he now saw his ex-wife. She was talking to some people who were concealed behind a man who looked like the man who had come to the gallery on a bicycle but could not have been he because his time for being there had passed. When the man moved off to get more wine, Shurnas saw that the people to whom his ex-wife was talking were the couple who'd had the party on Jane Street. He grew alarmed at first, fearing their presence would undermine the mood of the place. But then he realized that there occasionally had to be some familiar people around, if only to re-establish that you yourself were familiar.

All at once his ex-wife spotted him and broke away from the couple. Looking a little wildly over his shoulder, she said, "Start these around," and pressed something dry and papery into his hand. At a glance, he saw she had given him two joints. "Nobody's getting into my paintings," she said. "Maybe a little smoke will open up their heads." Shurnas watched her dart off. He thought about what had happened; it didn't take long for him to believe he had been exploited. Was he her servant? Or maybe she imagined the two of them were still allied. In any event, it was clear that since she had withheld her thinking from him, he had earned the right to keep the joints. Putting them in his shirt pocket, he turned to the couple as they rushed over to say they had missed him the other night.

Again, the information was terribly incomplete. Had "missed" been intended to tell him they thought he hadn't been at the party or that they'd failed to see him while he was there? It seemed to Shurnas that there was only one answer he could give.

"It was really a hot one," he said.

This of course implied nothing in particular, but at the same time it could imply almost anything. The couple could think he was saying it had been too hot a night to go to a party; or perhaps that he found conditions at their place too hot to stay long enough to be seen by them; or even, irrelevantly, that the party itself had been hot, in the sense of wild and exciting. Too late he saw that he had trapped himself into giving them an opening to say something about Jackie. "Yes, wasn't it unbearable? One poor woman who was at the party even died from the heat after she went home."

Though neither member of the couple said anything like that, Shurnas thought they were both looking at him as if they had. "I read about it," he heard himself say. He expected that would bring another look from them, but instead they both began talking about how the papers were full lately of nothing but the weather. Someone nearby, overhearing their discussion, said, "It's as if the sky is snowing blood." But when Shurnas wheeled around he couldn't figure out who had made the remark. Nice seeing the two of you are still able to be friends, the couple said. On the surface, it was a simple reference to Shurnas being at his ex-wife's opening, but he was too busy remembering something Jackie had once told him to respond. What had she meant by claiming she was too "down to earth" for him?

He walked out of the gallery, but after seeing his car was still there he went back inside. He stood in front of the portrait of himself, nudging the girl beside him with his elbow so she would make a little more room for him. She was telling the rather effeminate boy with her about a novel she was reading called *A Rose Is a Rose Is a Rose*. To Shurnas the title sounded like a bad joke. Nevertheless he could not get it out of his mind. Each time he repeated it to himself it threatened to go on and on without end. Once or twice, in talking, the girl bumped her hip lightly against his, but instead of the softness he had been looking forward to, the hip felt surprisingly angular. Then, when the girl interrupted her discussion of the novel to say, "This painting sucks," he began hearing a decidedly masculine timber in her voice.

Why hadn't he left the gallery when he went outside awhile ago? The notion that even though it was pointless for him still to be there he continued to be there was so disconcerting that he could no longer tolerate himself. The gritty feeling inside his clothes attacked him again. He immediately began scratching himself. Then, realizing how comical he must look—"Like a dog with fleas"—he stopped that and stood with his hands clenched at his sides. Each beat of his heart seemed to come right on top of the beat before it, as if the operation was one incessant hammering. The gritty feeling, his ex-wife, the couple who'd had the party, *A Rose Is a Rose Is a Rose*, then the gritty feeling again and his heart beginning to race—only now did Shurnas realize that although he desperately hoped these things were not connected, he was desperately seeking a connection. It had become so noisy in the gallery that he could no longer single out any one noise from the rest; and because, in contrast, everything inside him had grown very quiet, he no longer felt his heart. He held his breath.

In a moment, hearing a voice call his name, he tried to tell himself he didn't know, when he turned around, that Jackie was going to be right behind him.

She was wearing a tennis outfit: white shorts and a crimson tank top. Between it and her dark hair and her muscular legs, she looked like a Russian woman distance runner. "Fancy meeting you here," she said. Shurnas said nothing of his own whimsies. He murmured something about it being his ex-wife's opening. "Oh, which one is she? I've always wanted to meet my competition." Nervously, Shurnas tried to leave, but he stopped short when Jackie said, very softly, "Do you still remember how special that night was?"

52

Some while later she asked him if he was the man in the painting. Shurnas hadn't been answering very many of her questions up to that point, but after she said, "It doesn't begin to do you justice," he told her she wasn't too bad-looking herself. He began making other remarks that were meant as compliments in an attempt to get her off the subject of his ex-wife. Jackie persisted in referring to her as his wife. "There's no such thing as an ex," she said when he tried to correct her. "A wife is a wife."

Fearing she was going to add another "is a wife" to her statement, Shurnas hastily said, with a glance at his watch, that he had to run.

Not until he was out on the street did he notice that Jackie was still beside him. "How come you never called me again?" she asked. "Did you lose my number?" He would have showed her his address book to prove that he hadn't, but he wasn't sure but what her name might have been one of those he'd crossed out. Now that he had his key ring in his hand, he realized that he'd walked around to the passenger's side of his car as if to unlock the door so Jackie could get in. Despite having given himself away, he tried to pretend he didn't know what she was talking about when she said she hadn't known he had a car. Eventually, as she began running her fingers admiringly over the chrome, he said it wasn't really his. For proof he was going to show her the title, hoping she wouldn't notice what the manager had written on the back of it, but she was already getting into the car. It was then that he saw he had committed still another oversight: in parking the car he'd somehow neglected to lock the door on her side. Right away, merely in having thought the words "her side," he realized that he had irrevocably compromised himself. As he got into the car on the driver's side—pointlessly avoiding thinking of it as "his" side—she asked whether he minded running her uptown. But before he could answer she changed her request to an invitation to come up to her new place for a drink. Shurnas, who remembered too well how drinks with her never turned out to be drinks, nevertheless heard himself say, "I didn't know you'd moved," instead of the refusal he'd prepared himself to hear.

From behind the compact mirror she'd taken out of her shoulderbag, Jackie said, "That's not quite the right word." As they went up First Avenue, she explained that she still had her old place but recently had begun spending most of her time at her lover's apartment in the Sutton Arms. Shurnas didn't have to pretend that he'd never heard of the Sutton Arms. He saw her smiling at him—and somewhat at herself too in the compact mirror—when he went to shift gears. "Aren't you going to ask if he's married?" she said.

Shurnas should have said her personal life was no concern of his, but he noticed she was now wearing a gray cardigan over the tank top. Had that come out of the shoulderbag too? Amazingly, there was an empty parking place just a few blocks from the Sutton Arms. After pulling into it, he made absolutely sure this time before getting out of the car that all the doors were locked, there were no hydrants around and the sign really said the parking place was legal. He observed that, since tomorrow was a day that alternate side of the street parking regulations were suspended on the Upper East Side, the parking place was actually good until eleven o'clock two mornings from now. Before he could wonder what the hitch was, Jackie took his arm and began pulling him along the street. Walking beside her, he was aware that they must look like a typical couple to others, but the picture was not as distressing to him as it would have been under more typical circumstances. It seemed to Shurnas that being seen like this might even be valuable.

Just before they got to the Sutton Arms, Jackie told him to go on ahead for a minute. When he looked back he saw she had taken an orange wig out of her shoulderbag and was fitting it over her own hair. She didn't give Shurnas any explanation until they had passed the doorman and were waiting for the elevator. Then, in a whisper, she told him that people in the building were supposed to think she was her lover's wife who was a strawberry blonde. All of this intrigue excited Shurnas a little. He was beginning to understand it might even be possible to get in the mood for a good time.

In the elevator Shurnas was able to smile when Jackie gave him a conspiratorial wink on the ride up: it was fun to think they were in league against the rest of the building. But when he saw that they were going all the way up to the penthouse he grew tense. "You're really moving up in the world," he said as Jackie unlocked the door of her lover's apartment. Even though the remark was made half seriously, she laughed as though all she'd heard was an attempt to be funny. And in fact, once they entered the apartment and Shurnas saw how grandly it was furnished, the situation did begin to seem as if it might even become amusing.

Some of his tension returned when she took the orange wig off her head, tossed it on a basket chair in the living room and went out on the terrace. Seeing her dark hair again reminded him that he wasn't here with a woman of intrigue—he was here with Jackie. "No illusions this time," he told himself, though it seemed uncanny to him how she could be a stranger one moment and the next moment seem totally familiar. Silently he warned himself to forget it, it was notions like this that were causing all the trouble. Still, when Jackie leaned over the ledge that enclosed the terrace and said, "You won't believe this view," he was careful not to stand too close to her.

It was twilight. While the sky still had more of the colors of day than of night, the street far below was deep in shadows. The cars on it looked like a procession of small boxes. It bothered Shurnas to have to describe boxes as being in a procession because a word like procession implied movement and

55

boxes could not move of their own accord, but since the cars were very obviously in motion he could not get away with just calling them boxes. The terrace itself defied description: he was afraid if he allowed himself to look at too much of it he would see a tennis court. Already he could not keep from wondering if, because they were up so high, balls would feel lighter. After a while he wanted the sun to set and get rid of what little daylight lingered; in the dark the terrace could become a terrace again and the cars on the street below, visible only as a string of headlights, would no longer seem like boxes.

He started pacing because Jackie was now sitting on the ledge. As always when she made an irrational request, he felt it coming even before she said it. Why should he hold her feet? he inquired. In a moment, kneeling on the terrace in front of her, he asked himself whether it was inescapable, whether he wouldn't be wise simply to surrender to events and get it over with. He grabbed her ankles and when she disappeared backwards over the ledge so that all he could see of her was her legs, the muscles of which stood out like wales with the strain of supporting the rest of her body—which, not being able to see, he could only imagine dangling in space—he began holding his breath also. All he had to do was let go of her ankles: it could be that simple. Then he felt the muscles in Jackie's legs tighten like pulleys and lift her back into a sitting position on the ledge. For a woman, he had to admit, she was in terrific shape.

"You ought to try it," she said as soon as she returned to view. "It really clears out the cobwebs." Had he just passed a test? Everything indicated this, and such an interpretation immediately seemed reassuring. All in all, it felt to Shurnas as if his meeting Jackie in the gallery, his driving her uptown, his coming up here to her lover's apartment, his holding on to her ankles, were in the nature of trials. He stood up and looked out over the roof tops at the final smudges of daylight. As if to prove he could still get out of there anytime he wanted, he left the terrace, walked straight through the apartment to the front door, opened it and stepped out into the hall. It was that easy to do. Of course, having shown himself that he could get out of there, it was no longer necessary to get out of there.

Jackie was in the kitchen fixing two cool-looking drinks when he returned to the apartment. He stood behind her and rubbed the back of her neck awhile. Then, feeling her body begin to relax, he took his hand away — everything was still all right.

Just to doublecheck, he slipped his hands under her arm pits and cupped her breasts. That quickly, she said, "All you have to do is touch me." Shurnas, who was feeling pleased that he was not aroused in the least, at once remembered how easily she was aroused. He tore his hands away from her and went into the living room. There he turned on all the lights and sat in one of the two basket chairs that were on either side of the sofa. Looking around, he felt almost at ease when he saw nothing to disturb him. Then he noticed the orange wig on the other basket chair, and this was no longer true.

After a while Jackie came in with their drinks. She had changed from her tennis outfit to a scarlet shift that smelled so strongly of perfume that Shurnas couldn't distinguish her own musky athletic smell from it when she sat on the end of the sofa as close as possible to his chair. "Where do you go when you disappear?" she wanted to know. There was no way out of it; now that they were having a conversation events were going to involve him again.

Shurnas pretended to look elsewhere in the room when she held her drink up as if to begin a toast. His own drink was still on the table. He refused to touch it because of the effect alcohol could have on an empty stomach. "Still playing a lot of tennis?" he heard her ask. When he merely shrugged, still

57

without looking at her, she said, "Well, I finally broke down and admitted I'd better get my act together." She took a sip of her drink, then told him not to worry, her therapist could turn out to be his best friend. Irritated by all of her clichés, Shurnas looked at his watch. He actually got to his feet, but when he saw that Jackie had risen right along with him as if hoping his movement meant they were going to embrace, he sat down again. "What're you experiencing right now?" she said. Knowing she was not going to quit talking in clichés until she got him to say one, he nearly told her to give him a break.

His emotional state corresponded, now that he had begun intercepting the intense looks she was throwing him, almost exactly with the one that had impelled him once to agree with her when she told him he was the kind of person who needed a lot of space. He felt smothered. Within the looks she gave him he saw her eyes trying to pull his own into them as if to swallow him. Again he regretted having touched her in the kitchen. "You can't do anything they can take as encouragement," he thought. It was like electricity. Once turned on, it had to go somewhere. Therefore he wasn't surprised when she slid the shift off her shoulders and exposed her breasts; the nipples, flaccid when they first appeared in view, quickly stiffened. Faced with them, Shurnas could imagine nothing he wanted to see less—not even the orange wig. It went out of focus when he heard her say, "Am I still the only woman you've known who can come just from having them touched?" Suddenly he could no longer breathe. Also, his ankle was hurting from sitting too long in the same position.

Like her nipples—of which he was so acutely aware that her breasts looked flat, although they were considerably larger than average—all the small details of her body seemed to distort the broader ones that surrounded them. The only protection was to give them names that were opposite of the function they served. Thus her nipples were dents, as on a car fender,

58

and her navel was a hood ornament. And the tuft of pubic hair he began seeing as she pulled the shift down over her hips was an engine block. Even her legs, which did not really exist in relation to any other part of her and indeed were one of the broader details, needed another name. When none occurred to him, he realized this was because of the many different functions they served: walking, forming a lap while sitting, acting as leverage during lovemaking, sometimes being used to get and give messages as when you kicked somebody under the table. All at once the whole line of thought seemed senseless. How had he gotten started on anything so dumb? Oh, right, he'd been watching Jackie's nipples. And before that he had compared the sexual impulse to electricity. And on back he had been conscious of her staring at him.

Speaking of which, what had happened to the orange wig?

When he looked for it, he saw that Jackie, in the midst of his trying not to pay attention to her, had put it on her head again. "Now you can pretend I'm someone else," she said. Shurnas, who loathed fantasy and yet sometimes thought he lived on little else, knew he had to get the wig away from her. But when he reached for it the movement made her think he wanted to resume touching her, and she grabbed his hands and clapped them over her breasts.

It was the kind of struggle he couldn't win. Every time he got one hand away from her, she used the hand of hers that was now free to grab some other part of him. In order to get that part loose—his belt, say—he had to use his own free hand, and that gave her a chance to grab it again. Eventually things began tumbling out of his shirt pocket; some coins at first, and then the two joints he'd been given by his ex-wife. Seeing them, Jackie let go of his hands and cried, "Oh wow, jays! Get some matches!" Shurnas, who had forgotten he had the joints, almost blacked out when he stood up. He realized part of the problem was not having gotten much food in himself lately.

There was a box of matches on the kitchen stove, but when he returned to the living room with it Jackie had already lit one of the joints with a table lighter that appeared to be solid gold. "These people know how to live," Shurnas told himself. He sat down on the basket chair again, and Jackie handed the joint to him. After it was finished she began to touch her breasts. "Kiss me, I'm coming," she announced. Shurnas just sat there at first when she jumped on top of him, but when she tried to kiss him he turned his head away. "Like high school," she said. After a while she got off him and lit the second joint.

Shurnas heard a noise outside as if a branch had broken off a tree and fallen on the terrace. But there were no trees out there, so that was impossible. As soon as he had taken a puff of the second joint, he no longer felt like going out on the terrace to investigate. Later he sat inertly while Jackie removed his clothes. One or the other of them put the orange wig over the glass containing one or the other of their drinks so that from the back it looked like somebody's head discreetly not watching them. The conversation Jackie was making was loud; over it, the branch sounds on the terrace could be heard only occasionally. Every now and then he got an inkling of an erection. Encouraged, Jackie pounced on his lap. But he kept falling asleep.

After she finally had left him alone—"You really know how to leave a woman up in the air," he seemed to hear her say— Shurnas gradually woke up. He saw her come in from the terrace and turn off all the lights in the living room except the one behind his chair. Sitting in the shadow of himself that it cast, he said he wasn't budging. "What?" Jackie said, as if the word was foreign to her. But he was too smart to be lured into repeating it. In a while he fell asleep again. When he awakened he wasn't on the basket chair any longer; he was lying on the sofa. He thought about getting up, but he couldn't think of anywhere to go if he did. Then he realized he must have already gotten up: else how had he moved from the basket chair to the sofa? The knowledge that he had budged after vowing he wouldn't was depressing—as if he'd lost a contest with himself. Shurnas wanted to escape having to brood over his defeat by going back to sleep, but Jackie was still there. When he tried to get into a comfortable position on the sofa, she forced him to make room for her beside him. Later, dozing a little, he felt her hand stubbornly massaging his penis. Shurnas should have pretended he was asleep. But he had just enough marijuana in him to go along with her a ways.

Once she got his penis inside her, she wanted him to pick her up and carry her. And once he was staggering around the room with her clinging to him like a dead weight, she wanted him to put her down someplace where she could sit with her legs over his shoulders. Gradually it began to seem as if his body was not only joined to her body but was being ruled by it. Each slight movement he made was matched by some kind of overwhelming movement from her. Absorbed in avoiding the feeling that his body was in competition with hers, he caught himself counting to himself under his breath: "One one thousand...two one thousand...three one thousand..." It was distressing because what did time have to do with this event? *Time?* Shurnas interrupted his count. "What is time but a trick to keep everything from happening at once?" Once, right before his eyes, he'd seen this question scrawled over a restroom urinal.

The manner in which he got from the living room onto the terrace was as dim a memory to him as the manner in which he had moved from the basket chair to the sofa. Whenever he smoked marijuana the same kind of thing happened: one moment jumbling with another. "Under the influence of drugs." Anyway, it was an excuse for believing he was on the verge of gaining the power of flight. He must be going to try it because he was standing near the ledge and holding his arms straight out at his sides like wings. Only Jackie, who still had her legs and arms clamped around his waist, prevented him from taking off. Still hoping he could get free simply by reasoning with her, he told her, leaning over the ledge, that she was getting too heavy. But she wouldn't listen. Every time he tried to break her grip on him she only held on more tightly. Eventually he gave up struggling and started tickling her. It caused her hands to become occupied with stopping his. After that he gave her a push. He heard her scream, but it ended so quickly that he found himself craving other sounds.

Staring out over the ledge at the spot where he had last seen Jackie, he had a view of the windows on the upper floors of the buildings across the street. Many of them were lit, but looking into them he could not see anyone looking back at him. When he glanced up at the sky, he realized how relieved he was that he did not see Jackie. It was a little surprising that in all the time her body had been attached to his she too hadn't acquired the ability to fly. Shurnas froze. "The reason the killer will inevitably be caught is because he believes he's divinely inspired," someone had said in one of the articles he'd read about the jogger murders.

He was irritated to discover how little mess there was to clean up in the apartment: the pillows on the sofa hardly even needed to be straightened, the glasses they had drunk out of only had to be wiped off with a paper towel, the roaches from the two joints they had smoked could too easily be flushed away. It seemed to Shurnas that despite all the care he'd taken against planning ahead he had once again planned ahead. As he started to dress he felt better when he saw his clothes had left a few grains of sand on the carpet. Then, for no apparent reason, he went into the bathroom and turned on the shower. The pipes gurgled but no water came out. Shurnas made himself tell himself it was nothing personal: in a penthouse apartment the water pressure naturally took a long time to rise. In a while a few drops of water came out of the shower nozzle. This teased Shurnas into waiting longer. The floor of the shower stall was covered with black lines, a pattern of squares and rectangles on the tile that looked like a maze. All of the lines, no matter which route his eyes took, seemed to lead to the drain and end there. Unable to get his eyes past the drain, Shurnas suddenly felt menaced and at the same time protected. *Which* was more disturbing? Trying to think of a way to get out of the grip of both sensations, he spotted the orange wig. Hurriedly he put it on his head and left the apartment.

Taking the stairs all the way down to the first floor he encountered no one, but when he arrived in the lobby he saw a police car in front of the building. The red light on top of it was flashing. He went back into the stairwell, climbed up to the second floor and sat down on the landing. He removed his shirt, which already smelled rather strongly of perspiration, and used it to wipe his forehead. The air in the stairwell was so close that he began perspiring again almost immediately. Realizing that he was in danger of falling asleep if he stayed there, he returned to the lobby where he noticed that the doorman who was now on duty was not the same one who had seen him come in with Jackie. Also, the police car had gone. Shurnas's eyes grew heavy. Not only was it late at night, but the lamps in the lobby seemed excessively dim, as if the management of the Sutton Arms was trying to conserve energy. He waited until the doorman's back was turned, then left the building. At first he was startled that it was broad daylight, but then he understood that he would have been more startled if it had not been.

While walking away from the building, he saw someone moving toward him and recognized a man he had once given a lesson on serving. And when the man scurried past him without a look of recognition, it was not because he was in disguise under the orange wig but because he was no longer disguised as a tennis pro. Then and there Shurnas decided he had been given his chance to begin anew. On the next corner he stopped at a pay phone and was actually in the midst of looking through his pockets for a dime before he grew aware of what he was doing. A few minutes later he caught himself buying a newspaper. Since it would always be permissible to keep track of the date and the weather, this maneuver was not completely intolerable. Nevertheless, to avoid any further backsliding, he hailed a cab and went to the Plaza Hotel, the last place in the city he could imagine feeling at home and therefore the most logical place to go now. When it turned out the Plaza had no rooms, he asked the desk clerk to recommend another "acceptable" hotel in the area and was given the name of the Olcott on West 72nd Street. Convinced as soon as he left the Plaza that the desk clerk had suggested the Olcott because he got a commission for sending any overflow from the Plaza there, Shurnas went instead to a hotel on West 57th Street, where a woman who used to fly in from Houston to visit him had once stayed. As the hotel had been remodeled from top to bottom since her last visit, it had none of the dreadful familiarity; even its name had been changed from that of a Midwestern state to that of a Northeastern state.

In the lobby Shurnas realized he was still wearing the orange wig. He looked around for a place where he could remove it in privacy before registering for a room. Beyond the elevator bank was a sign that said *Bar*; knowing there would be a restroom in the bar, he started toward the elevators. As he passed the first one, the door opened and a tall black woman in a red caftan emerged. She was slightly too old for him, but when she mistook him for someone named "William" he readily pretended he was this William in her life. In the bar he talked to her over a drink, then went into the restroom to remove the wig. When he came out she asked him worriedly if he'd seen a redheaded man in the restroom. Later, wearing the wig again, he gave her a glimpse of his key ring. With a betrayed look she asked him if this meant he now had his own place. In a way, he said. She told him not to be silly. "You're still staying with me." A waitress came over to their table to see if they wanted another drink. It was astonishing to Shurnas how little of his first drink was left. He quickly ordered a Coke. Then he remembered that was no longer allowed and changed his order to milk. "And two eggs over easy." When the waitress said all they had were sandwiches, the woman tugged his sleeve to get his attention and then told him not to spoil his appetite because they were going out to dinner. "At the Vietnamese place on Eighth Avenue that you like so much."

The woman's room was on the ninth floor. She handed him her key as they got out of the elevator. When he waited for her to go ahead of him so he would know which direction to take, she linked arms with him and said, "Pleasure beckons." Glancing at the gold number engraved on the leather thong attached to the key, he saw they were headed for Room 909. That struck him as so meaningful that when his arm grazed the woman's hip as they were walking down the hall he allowed himself to feel aroused.

Room 909 faced the street; so many traffic noises could be heard that the woman turned on the TV set to override them. The picture on the set was very faint as if a tube was about to go. Between the hazy look of the TV screen and the air conditioner, which had an annoying rattle as if something was caught in the fan blades, Shurnas began to feel oppressed. While sitting on the bed watching the woman change from the red caftan to a white linen pants suit, he tried to tell her he wanted to take a shower but couldn't get her to listen. Every time he started to speak she stopped what she was doing to change the channel on the TV set. The picture kept getting fainter and fainter. He picked up the phone and asked for room service. When the woman overheard him ordering a pizza, she said, "Perhaps we have been eating out too much lately." She took the phone out of Shurnas's hand and said something into the receiver in French. He assumed she was requesting some exotic type of wine, but when the bellhop arrived with the pizza there were two bottles of Coke beside it on the serving cart. The room seemed to get even smaller.

A police siren on the street outside pierced the sounds from the TV set and the air conditioner as they were eating. "They're after you," the woman said. At first, although he was still wearing the orange wig, Shurnas thought his identity had been penetrated. Then, from her next remark, he realized she still believed he was William, who apparently was a somewhat antisocial character in his own right. Had he been staying out of the park?

If Shurnas had taken off the wig, the sight of him might have driven the woman to throw him out, but as it was, she just went on eating and talking as if he were someone she had known for years. At one point she said, "You're always going to be the kind of man I can dress up but can't take anywhere." A few minutes after that she told him merely being in the same room with him still gave her such a charge that she could barely swallow her food. Just the same, when Shurnas attempted to put his arm around her after they'd finished eating, she ignored it and got up to change the channel on the TV set.

While they were watching a *Starsky and Hutch* re-run, she went into the bathroom. When Shurnas heard the shower running he wanted to leave, but it seemed much too late to try to get a room of his own in the hotel that night. He tore off the orange wig, threw it under the dresser and then turned out all the lights and got into bed with his clothes on. The woman had a towel around her head when she came out of the bathroom. She asked Shurnas if he minded if she left her curlers in, and he lied saying that to tell the truth he was too exhausted for anything she did to make a difference. Before getting into bed she offered him a piece of chocolate candy from a heart-shaped box on the bedside table. That made him feel better, although he worried about going to sleep without brushing his teeth. His ankle felt more painless than not. When he mounted her, her vagina made a farting sound. Instead of being embarrassed she laughed and said, "Pussy's talking to you." Afraid he would come too quickly, Shurnas reminded himself that his name wasn't really William. After a while the woman asked him if the pizza had disagreed with him.

CHAPTER FOUR

Sometime in the night the air conditioner broke down completely.

After the woman got up to open the window, the traffic noises made it impossible for either her or Shurnas to get back to sleep. Eventually she turned on the TV set and watched a movie with Claire Trevor and two actors who both looked — although with the picture so hazy, it was perhaps unfair to make any claims about anyone's appearance — like Alan Ladd. By the time *Good Morning America* came on, Shurnas was so tense with wondering what she would do when it was light enough in the room for her to see that he wasn't William, that he drank part of a warm bottle of Coke left over from last night's dinner. But when at last she looked at him it was only to say he was lucky that sugar didn't make his face break out.

Shurnas put the Coke bottle down and lay in a pool of his own perspiration. No matter which way he moved the mattress was soggy, and he watched himself gradually break out in goose bumps. The woman showed no inclination to get started on the day. When he picked up the phone, she once again took it out of his hand. In English she asked for room service, then switched to French in ordering breakfast. Shurnas was stunned when two steaming pans that contained steaks smothered in mushrooms arrived a few minutes later. As long as the steaks remained covered, they'd still be warm if he wanted to take a shower first, she said.

He thought, "What else is new?" but after that there was an interruption in the pattern. Sitting on opposite corners of the bed, Shurnas and the woman ate without any small talk. Occasionally he glanced at her. The expression he saw on her face was so unreadable that she took on a peculiar wisdom, as if because everything about her was so unfathomable there could be nothing she did not know. Were she to call him William again, he would not have had the slightest doubt that his name was William. Had she told him it was cold in the room, the moisture he felt on his forehead and saw on hers would not have been perspiration but ice. Even though the piece of steak in his mouth was so tender that it melted like butter, he would have begun chewing like mad if she had said it was tough.

Suddenly, as a fly landed on the bed, the woman came to life. She raised her hand to swat it. Shurnas, finding her movement an interruption in his mood, was relieved when the fly disappeared before her hand could complete its motion. It wouldn't be summer without them, he heard her say.

And though he tried to relax, he knew it was hopeless—they were about to undergo another one of those conversations. Watching her lips open, he felt his own fighting to remain closed. He forced himself to smile gamely at her. Will it ever let up? she wanted to know. She then made some other comments about the weather than unsettled him. To shut her up he said, "It's as if the sky is snowing blood." Immediately his smile seemed to thaw. Motionless in front of the mirror on the dresser, he watched himself, hardly able to stop himself from laughing as in a dream when a moment of overpowering dread is repeated so often it becomes ludicrous. In talking to him now the woman seldom looked at him. Her way of telling him that she realized he wasn't William was to pinch his arm every now and then as if to test whether he had a reality in his own right. Shurnas expressed his awareness of the situation by making an "umm-m" sound each time she pinched him in order to show her that he had at least as good a grip on reality as she did.

The woman also talked a lot to the TV set; every time a commercial came on she argued with the actors who were extolling the virtues of this product or that one: "*Fab* schmab…*Rheingold* swinegold…*Wheaties* skeeties…" Of course the morning was passing vacuously, but Shurnas realized there were things he could do to keep it from being completely wasted. Sitting up in bed and gazing into the mirror on the dresser, he made faces at himself until he hit upon one that he had never seen himself do before. Later he smoked a cigarette just to see what effect it would have on his pulse rate. When the woman ignored him and went on talking to the TV set, he realized he had never been concerned enough about who he was because no one had told him how impossible it would be to become somebody else. "The more things change, the more they remain the same." For the first time it occurred to him that all of the expressions he was in the habit of uttering to himself were not necessarily meaningless just because he thought they were meaningful. To his disappointment, this notion seemed meaningless to him; which meant, since he now had a higher opinion of his own perceptions, that it probably was meaningless. Yet he recognized that there might still be a flaw in his reasoning. Would it be true to say that the less things changed, the less they remained the same? If not, what then?

Shurnas resented it when the woman stopped pinching his arm. Concerned as he was that she might leave marks, he could have endured her pinches forever in preference to having her talk to him. In a while he realized that the reason she had taken her hand off his arm was so she could pick up the box of chocolate candy on the bedside table. Her other hand was occupied with the fly which had begun pestering her again.

When she didn't offer Shurnas any candy this time, he was thankful. Why in the past had he let himself be blackmailed into feeling dismissed when others did not share their possessions with him? Then he realized he was now being blackmailed into feeling thankful. He asked the woman if he could turn off the TV set so he could hear himself think; she told him she had to go to Trinidad for a few days and he'd have to stay in her room while she was gone so they wouldn't take it away from her. "Who're they?" When her only reply was to shrug and reach for another piece of chocolate candy, the whole plot made complete sense to Shurnas. While she was packing he allowed himself a glimpse of the contents of her closet. Since she was tall many of the clothes she was leaving behind looked as if they would fit him. He had the feeling, watching her get into a pair of brush blue jeans, that he had once had an identical pair.

When she was gone, he started to take the clothes he had been wearing to a cleaners around the corner from the hotel, then reversed himself and threw them in a dumpster after being careful this time not to leave his keys in the pockets. From sleeping most of the night in an air-conditioned room, he would have expected his neck to be stiff, but it felt fine. He noticed, though, in walking, that his ankle still wasn't quite right.

On the elevator ride back up to the woman's room, he felt the operator was trying to catch his eye. Certain the man was about to offer him a prostitute, he got off the elevator on a lower floor and raced down the stairs to the lobby. There he saw that someone had left an early edition of the *Post* on one of the lounge chairs. In leaving the hotel he had to keep his eyes on the floor to avoid seeing the headline. Once outside, he realized his movements were in danger of becoming a parody of themselves. Nothing could possibly have happened to Jackie. To prove that the other night had been nothing more than his imagination at play, he took a cab to the Sutton Arms and recklessly got out of it right in front of the building. When he tried to enter the lobby, the doorman stopped him. Is this the place where that woman fell off her terrace? he demanded. The doorman's face was blank, but his hands appeared to tremble for a moment. Of course this reaction could be taken to mean that the doorman, as part of his job, was trying to protect the reputation of the Sutton Arms. Nevertheless Shurnas convinced himself that the doorman was not quite successfully masking that he had been caught off balance by an absurd inquiry. To make sure, Shurnas knew he ought to repeat his question, but the doorman was beginning to look familiar. Or was it not simply that he had been there too long by now for the doorman still to be a stranger?

Shurnas realized that he owed it to himself to get into the Sutton Arms so he could check whether it too looked familiar, but he was not going to let himself become panicked. Once he started doubting a conclusion he had reached, it was too easy to convince himself that he was not convinced. So he walked around the neighborhood awhile, bought a hotdog and a can of soda off a cart on First Avenue, and then slowly, pausing every few steps to rest his ankle which had begun feeling sore again, he wandered on down the block where he had left his car the other night.

Since his watch indicated it was still fifteen minutes short of the hour by which his car had to be moved, he was not overly nervous—even though he had cut things a bit close, he still had plenty of leeway. At first when he didn't see the car, he assumed that his watch was wrong and the car had been towed away. For a moment the same reasonless panic swept over him that he experienced each time he discovered his tennis racket had somehow gotten into the wrong hand. As if in spite of all his care to keep every movement in its proper order, events still had gotten out of whack. Then he understood that since he had not been at the Sutton Arms the other night, his car was quite naturally not there either.

He walked to the end of the block and watched a woman approach him dragging a small dog on a leash. She asked him to hold the leash while she lit a cigarette. He asked her the time, concealing in his pocket the hand of the wrist with his watch on it. Nearly eleven, she said as she took the leash back from him. Smoke from her cigarette stung his eyes for a moment. When he turned around the uptown side of the block was entirely clear of cars except for one that was the same make as his but a different color. From where he was standing he could see a piece of paper under one of the windshield wipers that stuck straight up in the air like a sail. He imagined the paper was a parking ticket, but when he pulled it out from under the wiper blade he saw it was a flyer for an auto body shop that was running a special that week: a complete paint job for half price. A police tow truck turned the corner. Watching it, you felt a monster was coming. Rapidly Shurnas unlocked the door of his car and jumped in behind the wheel. As the tow truck passed him, the driver appeared to be smiling at something. Able to see where the situation would have an element of humor to someone in the driver's position, Shurnas did not get angry.

The body shop was on First Avenue. Although the manager pretended not to know what Shurnas was talking about when he said he had no intention of paying for a paint job he hadn't ordered, Shurnas glanced behind him several times to make sure he wasn't being followed as he walked back to his car; he expected someone to jump him at any moment. It was plain to him that the body shop had singled his car out as belonging to someone who did not know the system and attempted to pull a fast one.

He got into his car and slammed the door shut. No one tried to stop him as he drove off, but the manager of the body shop could be seen in the sideview mirror staring at him. And then, waiting for a traffic light, he saw himself in the rearview mirror staring at the headline of the newspaper under the arm of a man who was crossing the street in front of his car:

JOGGER KILLER CLAIMS FIFTH VICTIM

It was time suddenly to get out of town. Looking down at the key ring dangling from the ignition of the car, Shurnas realized that he still had a key to the woman's apartment on York Avenue. And he had left some clothes in a cleaners over her way. It was necessary to think of these things not as loose ends but as tasks he had been assigned. He parked his car, took the cleaning ticket out of his wallet and wrapped it around the woman's key. Now he had a bundle small enough to hide in the palm of his hand. He got out of the car and stood next to a sewer grate. He noticed how the longer he stood there, the more people seemed to be watching him. Eventually he knelt on the sewer grate as if to tie his shoe and opened his palm. In a moment he heard a splash. It was fortunate that there were enough traffic noises to cover it. He got back into the car, thought about the rest of the tasks he has been assigned, and realized that his only chance to get into his apartment without calling on his ex-wife for help had been thrown away with the cleaning ticket. True, his key had probably been lost in the cleaning process, but someone in his position could not afford to take anything for granted.

Everything about the car had become an encumbrance. The function it served was not to make his life easier but to take over his life. It was like a retarded child: you had to keep your mind on it every second. To get rid of it, he left it in a "No Standing" zone in front of the woman's hotel with the key in the ignition while he went up to her room to use the phone. The switchboard operator in the hotel told him there were no outside lines available at the moment; when she called back to report one had opened up, he said he liked her voice. It seemed he must be trying to flirt with her, but he could think of nothing to do with her reply that he sounded pretty sexy himself.

On the other end of the line then, a different voice: Hello? *Hello?* Much too deep to be his ex-wife, but when he checked to see if he had the number he'd dialed, he was told by the voice that he did. Then it crossed his mind that his ex-wife must have someone staying with her and he asked the voice to call her to the phone. No, nobody by that name here. He dialed the same number and got the same voice. By this time his own voice was getting a little unrecognizable. He willed it calm, then dialed information. When told by the information operator that his ex-wife had an unlisted number, he said he was aware of that—in fact, he'd once known it by heart, but today for some reason he'd mixed up a couple of the digits when he went to dial it. He explained how he'd crossed her number out in his address book after he'd gotten it firmly planted in his mind. Now, alas, there was an emergency and he needed it. The information operator said she sympathized with him, but sorry, there were strict rules.

Rules! Shurnas was furious. Then his rage subsided and he became panicked. After a while the panic gave way to depression, because he realized that he had counted on his ex-wife not only to have a duplicate key to his apartment but also to refresh him on the address. He called room service and had copies of the Manhattan telephone directory for each of the last three years brought up. When he did not find his name in any of them, he called information again and asked for his own phone number. Told initially that there was no listing for anyone by that name, he was relieved—if he couldn't keep track of himself, no one else could either—but then he heard himself being informed that a further check showed a Shurnas

75

on East 19th Street. Shurnas almost said it was a mistake, some fool had transposed east and west. In his distress he almost did not remember to get the address on East 19th Street from the information operator.

He noticed when he left the hotel that his car was no longer in front of it. But his sense of freedom was shortlived. No sooner did he set foot outside the front door than he felt a hand on his arm. When he turned someone in a security uniform yelled at him. What was wrong with him? Did he know how close he'd come to being towed away? Lucky for him the hotel had seen to it that his car was put in a garage down the street. Informed that the charge for the garage would be added to the woman's bill, Shurnas tried to walk away from the hotel, but his ankle throbbed so much that he had to sit down in the lobby for a minute. When he rose it was with an understanding that keeping the car awhile longer could be useful. Besides making it easier for him to get around, it precipitated a new identity. The title to it, still legally in a name that was not his but had the same initials as his, was a launching point. Now, where was it? To himself, as he rushed toward the garage, he said, "You're worse than the absent-minded professor."

Only when he'd found that he still had the cleaning ticket in his wallet did it occur to him that the paper in which he'd wrapped the key to the woman's apartment might have been the car title. Then he looked at the cleaning ticket again and saw the date on it was a year old. Although he tore the ticket up, he did not do it quickly enough to escape observing that the address on it was for an establishment on York Avenue. "Like a dog chasing its own tail," he said, and then immediately warned himself not to talk so candidly to himself.

The garage would not give him his car without a claim ticket. Eventually he convinced the attendant that a call to the hotel would straighten the matter out and hovered outside the attendant's office while he phoned. Unable to overhear the conversation, Shurnas understood, when the attendant stopped meeting his eyes through the office window, that the car had been his downfall. He stood rigidly still a moment, but then he had to sit down on a bench: his legs were shaking. The attendant hung up the phone and stuck his head out of the office; he made a hand signal that Shurnas did not know how to take. Shurnas sank deeper into the bench. The attendant came all the way out of the office to tell him that his car was "upstairs" and someone would be "down" with it in a minute. Shurnas started to reach into his pocket for a tip, but the attendant must not have known how to take Shurnas's hand signal either. With a shrug, he returned to his office.

After battling crosstown traffic for several blocks, Shurnas turned south on Fifth Avenue. He drove cautiously because he did not want to be stopped and asked for his license and registration this far along in the game. All of a sudden he realized he not only was missing both these documents but that he was also driving without insurance. It would be a legal pickle for all concerned if he had an accident.

On East 19th Street his car and a Cadillac driven by a man in a chauffeur's uniform arrived simultaneously at the same parking place. Not wanting to create an incident in his own neighborhood, Shurnas would have agreed to flip a coin for the parking place, but when the chauffeur got out of the Cadillac brandishing a lug wrench, he realized an amicable resolution might not be possible. The chauffeur told Shurnas to get out of his car and fight like a man. Shurnas thought he probably would, but then the chauffeur, who had on leather gloves as part of his uniform, appeared to have a change of heart. In any event, the chauffeur turned around very abruptly and walked away. Shurnas supposed the chauffeur had not liked the impression formed by all the towels spread on the front seat cover. One of them, he noticed now, had a blood stain on it. From the girl he'd met on the beach? She hadn't mentioned being in her period, but few women did anymore.

Unable to find his name on any of the mail boxes in the building whose address he'd been given by the information operator, Shurnas rang the superintendent's bell. In a long while an old woman in a babushka emerged from an apartment at the end of the first-floor hallway. Shurnas decided it was the babushka that made the woman look old. Actually she was probably around the same age as himself. For a moment, although he tried, Shurnas could not remember his own age; it wasn't all that important anyway, since he wasn't going to be himself much longer.

The woman did not recognize him, which was not astonishing—the clothes he was wearing hadn't had enough time to acquire any of his characteristics. He asked her if she had a master key to his apartment and handed her one of his cards. The woman looked at it: *M.R. Shurnas. Tennis Pro. Lessons by the hour or half hour.* When she nodded and started back inside the building, Shurnas assumed she meant for him to follow her. But she only went as far as a table in the front hall, where she opened the top drawer and removed an envelope. Giving it to him, she said, "This came awhile ago. Not having a forwarding address, I didn't know what to do with it."

Shurnas noticed the envelope had already been forwarded once from an address on Eldridge Street. He was going to demand that the woman explain how her building had moved from the west side of town to the east side, but she had already returned to her apartment. When Shurnas rapped on her door, she called through it that his being evicted had been none of her doing. Now Shurnas should have inquired about the circumstances under which he had been evicted. But he had just remembered that it was his ex-wife and not himself who lived on West 19th Street. When he opened the envelope the woman

78

had given him, a mimeographed note fell out. It was an invitation from his ex-wife to her new art exhibition. Shurnas knew enough by now not to look at the date on it.

He thought about going at once to the address on Eldridge Street, but he wasn't sure there were enough hours left in the day for what he would find there. Instead he went around the corner to a barbershop. There he had his hair cut and his mustache shaved off. Until he saw himself in the mirror with short hair he hadn't remembered that he had a mustache. When the barber recommended a new shampoo that had just come on the market, he bought a tube of it so he could stay in the chair awhile longer. The longer he sat there, the better were his chances that the barber would remember his present appearance over the one he'd had when he came into the shop. What bearing this would have on his future was unclear, but his instinct was it was one of the things you did if you were serious about looking for a new lease on life.

Although the woman's hotel was more than two miles from the barber shop, he walked to it because there seemed little hope that he could find a legal parking place for his car any closer than the one he had on East 19th Street. It did not occur to him that he could have taken a train to the hotel until he passed a subway entrance on Times Square. He was amazed at how quickly you began to think like a car owner. He was also a little surprised that his ankle no longer was bothering him, but he still felt compelled to remind himself that self-treatment could always have an unseen pitfall or two. The shadow cast by the woman's hotel covered every inch of the pavement in front of it by the time he got to West 57th Street. As he entered the lobby, he was upset when the shadow tried to follow him in the door, but then he saw it was only a reflection in the glass of his own shadow.

In Room 909 in the hotel he woke up a long while before dawn and noticed that he was hungry. He found something in the drawer of the bedside table that felt in the dark like food and put it in his mouth; it had a slight tobacco flavor but not bad. Later he finished the last of the box of chocolate candy. The light that came through the window was still very dim, but the curtain was blowing about as if there were rain in the air. All at once he realized he could not remember the last time it had rained, and now he understood. As if he were an amnesiac, one day was always going to seem the same as the next. "Like beads on a string." Or better, on a necklace—for no matter how many times your fingers went around the strand, they never ran out of beads to touch or escaped coming back to the one with which they'd started. In that moment he lost his longing to be rid of himself; the void it left was filled by a sense of calm that seemed almost familiar. He knew that he would never again need to feel that events progressed logically from one point to another, and that from now on only one thing mattered: to resign himself to repeating himself. "A man's character is his fate." And as though all of this had merely been another one of those notions that seemed meaningful one moment and meaningless the next, he caught himself saying, "Cliché! Utter complete cliché!"

He sensed that he was running late again. "Always behind schedule like the hare in *Alice in Wonderland*," he thought, but the comparison did not make him move from the bed. Before falling back to sleep he took a final look at his watch: it was five o'clock, and it came to him that he felt older now than he had a year ago. Therefore he must be older. Therefore a year must really have passed. He did not have to complete the rest of the syllogism because it was just a device his mind was using to put him back to sleep. Lying there on his back, he saw himself lying there on his back.

In a few minutes, realizing that he now saw himself seeing himself, he went into the bathroom and took a long shower.

The walk to East 19th Street from the hotel seemed shorter

this morning than the walk yesterday from East 19th Street to the hotel. As a point of information, Shurnas would normally have counted the number of steps it took, but his mind was too busy calculating whether he felt safest driving east to East Hampton, north to Boston, west to Pittsburgh or south to Washington. "East Hampton," he decided with relief upon realizing there might be messages in going to a place called East as opposed to going to places that began with syllables like Bos, Pitts and Wash. Moreover, East Hampton was on the water, which had certain other messages; and anyway, the letters in east form "eats"—a positive word—whereas those in north, south and west formed only negative words like thorn, shout and wets. Then he saw that west could also be rearranged so that it spelled "stew": on the surface a positive word, until he remembered that stew could have a meaning that had nothing to do with food.

On the Long Island Expressway, he noticed that traffic was lighter than he'd been led to expect from its reputation, although it was true that the pinging noises in his car got louder the faster he went. So, after weighing the two phenomena, there was no advantage one way or another—the breaks had come out exactly even. But wasn't he getting a little too concerned with looking for signs? All signs pointed to this, and there was the final proof: using the very word to describe the very condition he was trying to elude. Altogether it seemed to Shurnas as if his preoccupation with fate was an excuse for not taking a stand. He narrowed his eyes against the sunlight pouring in the windshield. "Captain your own ship," he muttered to himself. As if to mock himself, he immediately began refusing to pass all cars with out-of-state license plates.

As soon as he got to East Hampton, he told himself that he was supposed to be a new person and therefore should be looking into starting a new career. But then he remembered there was a school of thought that claimed the best place to hide was in plain sight. By noon he had made the rounds of all the private tennis clubs in town. There were too many. Ever since he had become a teaching pro Shurnas had been amazed that other people continued to maintain an interest in the sport but had never decided whether his feeling withal was pity for them or for himself. As with all his passions, tennis seemed a waste of time and yet so precious that he resented having to share it with anyone.

There was a job open at one of the clubs; a teaching pro had fallen off a horse only the day before and broken his leg. Shurnas knew even before he applied for the job that he would get it. Since he was too careful to trust in his own premonitions, he was not surprised when the manager told him they were looking for someone a little younger. Still he felt a vein pulsating in his neck as if in disappointment. But there were also indications that he was not disappointed. He didn't smile and he was thirsty. Anyway, he was listening when the manager said there was a crippled man in town with a private court who was willing to pay double the standard lesson rate to anybody who could beat his son. "If you lose," the manager told him, "all you're out is a couple of hours of your time. If you win, it's found money." As the boy was sixteen, the challenge was palatable to Shurnas because legally he did not have to think of the boy as a kid.

He drove to a section of town called Hampton Waters. The feeling that there might be rain in the air had long since vanished. Even though the area around Hampton Waters was heavily wooded, the sun still prevailed; a faint heat haze seemed to hang over the trees and not so much as a single leaf stirred on any of them. Shurnas slowed his car to a crawl when he recognized the dirt road the manager had described in giving him directions to the crippled man's house. At the end of the dirt road he saw a gravel driveway. He parked at the foot of it. Then he got out of the car, dug his tennis racket out of the back seat from beneath the newspaper the girl had thrown over it the other day and took his equipment bag out of the trunk. He changed into a tennis outfit behind a tree. The sun, even though he could see only a few rays of it through the tree tops above him, beat down on his head so fiercely that he could almost imagine it was singling him out. He stood as still as he could until he did not feel pursued anymore. A moment later, walking up the driveway toward the house, he realized that the angle of the front window was such that anyone looking out of it could have seen him changing behind the tree. In another moment he realized that a clean-shaven man in a tennis outfit and a bearded man in a wheelchair were in the window.

Even though they obviously saw him, it was impossible to get them to come out of the house; they just stared through the window at him. Shurnas seemed to see a tennis racket in the clean-shaven man's hand. Then again, it might only have been a reflection in the window of the tennis racket in his own hand. Then still again—the clean-shaven man might have been a reflection of himself. Shurnas was first struck by this possibility when he raised his right hand in a wave and the left hand of the clean-shaven man shot up. For further verification, Shurnas then shifted his racket from his left hand to his right hand and raised his left hand. When the right hand of the clean-shaven man went up, Shurnas began wondering if the bearded man in the wheelchair was also a reflection. He looked to his left—the direction in which the bearded man in the wheel-chair would have had to be since in the window he was to the right of Shurnas's reflection—but saw no one. When he returned his gaze to the window, however, a tall blond boy was standing to the left of his reflection. Actually not to the left of Shurnas's reflection but to the right of Shurnas himself—for Shurnas was aware now that someone other than he had hold of the handle of his tennis racket. Turning, he saw that the boy, at sixteen, was already well over six feet. What kind of strings did he have? the boy wanted to know. How come some of them were black? Until then Shurnas hadn't realized that the newsprint from the *Post*, which had lain on top of his racket in the back seat of his car, had rubbed off on the strings of his racket. "Things happen when you're on the road," he said.

In the meantime the bearded man had come out of the house. His wheelchair was powered by a small motor, but he spun the wheels with his hands as he led the way down a gravel path to the tennis court. Although the court had a concrete surface, Shurnas felt his feet sink into it a little when he stepped on it. The boy opened a new can of tennis balls, then asked Shurnas if he had brought any "decent" balls. After announcing to Shurnas that he was there merely as a spectator, the bearded man took up a position behind the court where he could "watch the lines" from his wheelchair. The sun was at noonday height, but most of the court was in shadows. Tied to the boy's forehead was something green that Shurnas at first thought was a band to absorb perspiration but then realized was a sponge that kept a steady trickle of water dribbling down the boy's face. During the warmup Shurnas found himself limping even though his ankle no longer hurt. "Go ahead and serve first," the boy said, then told Shurnas to spin his racket so they could determine which of them would serve first.

The bearded man, who once again insisted he was not there to umpire, nevertheless called a foot fault on Shurnas the first time he served. As if to demonstrate his impartiality, he refused to offer an opinion when his son called each shot of Shurnas's that landed on a line "out." You boys have the best view, he said. Later he gave the wrong score in the set and resolved the dispute by telling his son and Shurnas—who was ahead in games, 5-0—to play a tiebreaker. "For the championship of Hampton Waters."

On the first point of the tiebreaker Shurnas's serve was so

hard that it knocked the racket out of the boy's hand. At first the boy claimed not to have been ready, then he claimed the serve was no good. "Play one," he said. The strip of sponge across his forehead was starting to look orange. When Shurnas turned around and saw the bearded man had fallen asleep in his wheelchair, he asked himself what he was trying to prove here; he must have walked off the court before he answered himself. His tennis racket might have been in his left hand, but who could afford to look anymore?

The bearded man woke up in time to race Shurnas to his car. Shurnas should easily have been able to outrun a man in a wheelchair, but he was too afraid that someone was going to leap out from behind a tree and grope at him. When he got to the car, the bearded man was waiting to ask him if all the women who had taken up tennis were ruining it. Shurnas turned on the motor and backed quickly out of the driveway without looking behind him. Once he was on the road, he kept his eyes fixed straight ahead of him on the windshield but did not look in the rearview mirror. So long as he did not have to see himself seeing himself there was still hope the whole mess would not follow him out here in the country.

He tried to go to "Main Beach" in East Hampton but was told as he was getting out of his car that the police would tow him away since he didn't have a parking sticker. How could he get one? Well, that depended on whether he was a resident or a visitor. Shurnas, who wasn't about to think of himself as either one, drove to a smaller beach on the outskirts of East Hampton. There it was the same story. All these restrictions were making Shurnas a little frantic. Everywhere he went in his car he saw the ocean, but he could not seem to get out of one and into the other. He drove to the next town, Amagan-sett, where there were some more beaches that were off limits to cars without stickers. At one of them he was told he could park if he paid a two-dollar fee. When he argued the ocean should be free, he was made to understand it was—for people without cars! It was the same trap he thought he'd left behind in the city.

While waiting in line to buy a root beer float at an ice cream stand in Amagansett, he was overheard complaining about the conspiracy against car owners by a woman in a T-shirt that said *Born to Live/ Dying to Run*. She promised that she would show him a beach where he didn't need a sticker if he gave her a lift to her car in Montauk. Shurnas, who made it a practice never to pick up hitchhikers, could not really regard her as a hitchhiker because he had not been solicited for a ride but rather had been offered an exchange of services. "You stroke my back, I'll stroke yours," he thought, noticing that the logo on the woman's T-shirt was the same color as the dark circles of perspiration under her arms.

Shurnas should have known when the woman wanted to be taken to her car that it meant she had jogged the length of the highway between Montauk and Amagansett. He heard her tell him once they were underway that she was training for the women's mini-marathon in Central Park. Hadn't that been canceled because of all the murders? Having mentioned the word, Shurnas did not stupidly look at her to see how much she knew but cleverly looked in the rearview mirror to see if he could catch himself trying to see how much *he* knew.

When he was on the open highway, the pinging noise in his car once again got louder. "It sounds as if you've got a flat tire," the woman said. Shurnas, who thought the woman had told him he looked tired, sat up straighter in his seat. In a while she said, "If you keep driving on it, you'll ruin the rim." When he stopped the car, she got out and went behind a dune.

Assuming she had gone to relieve herself, Shurnas stayed in the car and drummed his fingers on the steering wheel. Finally he grew impatient and urinated in the plastic cup that had held his root beer float so he'd know how much longer to give her.

He hated mixing liquids like that, but you didn't always have your choice of instruments when you measured time. Climbing the dune to investigate, he found the woman sunbathing. She still had her running shoes on but was otherwise nude. Shurnas noticed in passing that the shoes were blue. "The tires are fine," he said. "It's in the engine." Turning over on her back, the woman said, "Five more minutes on my face." Her navel had sand in it. The longer Shurnas stood there, the more it seemed to him that the terrain around him did not differ from all the other places he had been: although there was no water as far as the eye could see, the dune made it feel as if water were imminent. At the same time it occurred to Shurnas that what he saw while staring at the woman was a surrogate for a woman. Nothing about her body could hold his attention. As though she was already so familiar to him that he could not help but be bored. His own body was also beginning to bore him because it was reacting familiarly to the circumstances in which it found itself.

He stood there awhile longer, then removed his clothes and sat down beside her. While he waited for her to tell him it was too hot for sex, he passed the time by looking for all the three-letter words in woman. Mow, man, maw, won, wan, now and own came to him quickly. Mown and moan seemed to be the only four-letter words. Ordinarily he would have been intrigued that both of them sounded alike, but now he became obsessed with finding a third four-letter word; it seemed wrong that there were only two. When he heard the woman tell him that blow jobs were nice, he immediately made blow into bowl. By thinking of the event as a bowl job maybe it wouldn't seem so inevitable. He looked up into the sky, where the sun was beginning to decline. The hour, judging by the shadows, was somewhere in the middle of the afternoon. Sure enough, his watch said three o'clock. So the time at least was orderly; on each occasion a bit earlier. Cars could be heard speeding along the highway on the other side of the dune as the woman motioned him to move out of the path between her and the sun. She didn't mind doing him, she said, but she might as well get in a few more minutes of tanning at the same time.

She spat on his penis, then wiped it dry with her T-shirt before putting it in her mouth. When she squatted over him, her breasts hung suspended like two balloons filled with water. Eventually she asked him to rub some coconut oil on her back, then got on top of him. He had an orgasm almost at once, but she went right on pumping. Six months ago she couldn't have done this, she said. Running might be boring, but it did wonders for the legs. A plane flew over them, filled the air with its sound for several moments and then disappeared into the horizon. The woman rolled off him and lay on her back doing the bicycle exercise. Listening to her count the repetitions in German, Shurnas had nowhere to look but at her blue running shoes, and he wondered if this was not rubbing a little too much salt into the wound.

As the time in each instance had grown progressively earlier, so the pain in his leg had moved progressively lower. Getting back into his car, Shurnas anticipated that his foot would start to act up. When his back felt as if someone had stuck a knife in it, he was terrified. Did it mean the principles of medicine didn't apply out here in the country? He would have told the woman that she had to drive because he'd popped a disc, but she was busily filing her nails. Had he ever noticed how the salt air made everything grow faster? she asked. When she picked up the copy of the *Post* that had been traveling around with him in the back seat of the car, Shurnas understood that he'd slipped up by not throwing it out. The front page was blurred from having rubbed off on the strings of his tennis racket, but the woman seemed to have no problem reading it. When he heard her talking about the model who'd taken a "swan dive," he asked her to please stop speaking in slang. He saw the woman's mouth close and her eyes open wide; after a moment she said, "*Ja, ja.*" For the remainder of the ride the woman went on talking as fast as ever, but since it was in another language he was not required to listen.

CHAPTER FIVE

None of the cars parked along the beach in Montauk had stickers. The woman had explained that the regulations out here were much looser because it was not really part of the Hamptons. "It's more your kind of place," she had said. Shurnas, who had told her nothing about himself, nevertheless concluded that she had his number. It was uncanny how much less impersonal women who amounted to nothing more than one-night stands were getting. But could an incident that happened in the afternoon be called a one-night stand? And the word stand—wasn't his use of it yet another example that he was being too dramatic? Why couldn't each incident simply be called an interlude? Or even left at incident? Wasn't he trying to make too much out of something that was really no more than a few minutes of recreation? As though he did not take any of this seriously but argued the point just for the sake of argument, he told himself, "What is sex if it's not a good time?" Then, seeing how easily that sort of statement could start another argument, he clapped his hands together, a gesture that he interpreted as a decision that the subject didn't merit any further thinking about. But when he went on talking to himself the interruption began to seem only a decision that there could be no decisions.

He left his car, walked down the road a few yards, then wheeled around and looked to see if the car was still there. "Force of habit," he muttered, though he wondered how something he had begun doing only a few days ago could already have attained the stature of a habit. And it upset him, much as he wanted to disengage himself from the car, that he was having to leave it behind. He walked onto the beach as though entering a no man's land. His movements, he realized, were furtive, as if he had no right to be there. It was all right to feel like a total stranger, but you couldn't let yourself look like one.

To give himself the appearance that he had a part in things he got into a volleyball game in front of a beachside bar that seemed to be a hangout for the summer college crowd. The ocean was reflected in the windowpane of the bar. Actually most of the reflection was of the sky; there were no clouds, and except for the fact that the sun was in the sky, he could make no distinction between it and the water. Both were blue and bright, both merged as one at the horizon. The scene was so unified that Shurnas had the sensation he was looking at an idealization of nature rather than at nature itself.

At one point, holding the volleyball in his hands because it was his turn to serve, he stared at the reflection of the ocean and the sky in the bar window—everything looked so far away that he felt the whole world had receded from him. Then an object that stuck straight up in the air like a sail drifted into the reflection. Turning from the window, he saw nothing in the ocean or the sky that corresponded to the object. When he brought his gaze back to the window, he realized that someone inside the bar, sitting on the other side of the window, must be looking at a menu. It confused him that he saw the menu so clearly but could make out no details of the person holding it. His legs began shaking. Then the shaking spread to his arms and he dropped the volleyball. A girl on his team picked it up and tried to return it to him; he blinked at her.

It had grown very bright on the beach. The shaking would not stop. Though the water glittered almost painfully, it was inviting. Beside him the sand crunched. Turning, he saw the girl had given the volleyball to a long-haired boy who was getting ready to serve in his place. "Excuse me, sir," the boy said.

Sir? Shurnas heard somebody nearby him draw a sharp breath.

The water did not relieve the shaking: it was too cold. Shurnas did not see how that could be possible with all the hot weather they'd been having. It almost seemed as if the water had made a fool of him, enticing him into itself with the promise of making him feel better and then reneging on its promise. He sat down on the sand and hugged his knees. After a while, realizing he was no longer shaking, he began to have a kinder opinion of the water. Perhaps it hadn't lied to him after all. Then he became amused at the way he'd attributed human motives to one of nature's elements. As long as he could still carry off stunts like that nothing could go too far wrong.

In a while he lay down on his back so the sun could dry him. For a few seconds this was pleasant, then he grew restless. He wasn't shaking any longer, so what was the point? From time to time, at a distance, he heard the sound of a fist thudding against the volleyball, followed by the cries of the players in the game. These noises only seemed to make him yearn for more noise.

He stood up and went to join a group of college kids waiting beside the volleyball court to challenge the winning team. They didn't seem thrilled to see him again. One of them, a boy in a red tank suit, told Shurnas there was a better crowd of players every afternoon at a private beach on the Old Montauk Highway. Shurnas took "better" to be a euphemism for older. "You need a car to get there," the boy added. Involuntarily, Shurnas glanced in the direction his car was parked, then took an apprehensive glance at his watch. As invariably happened when something he was told in the guise of information carried the possibility of an insult, he grew tense. What should his response be? In a moment the impulse to transform himself into someone else became a physical need, and he told the boy his name was William. Instantly he began to listen calmly as the boy gave him directions to the private beach. When the boy mentioned that someone would stop him at the entrance to the road leading to the beach and ask him for a password, it was no use denying he was excited. The password changed each day, the boy said, depending on what the big news story was in the sports world. Even though it had been several days since he'd last seen a sports page, Shurnas did not pretend to himself that he was surprised to learn today's password was "streak."

On the Old Montauk Highway he passed two girls on foot. Since they weren't hitchhiking, he stopped and asked them if they wanted a ride. One of the girls told him they were staying down the road at Gurney's Inn. Shurnas asked if that was a good place. She said it didn't have tennis. While he was deciding where this conversation was taking him, the other girl got into the car and smiled at him. "You're not a rapist or anything, are you?" she said. Shurnas realized then that he preferred her to her friend and reached across her to close the door so they could drive off alone; he was even going to invite her to go with him to the private beach. But she said she was trying to work up an appetite by walking and got out of the car.

Watching the two girls move off down the road, Shurnas promptly became aware of his own lethargic appetite. "That's what I should be doing," he thought. "Treating this as a vacation and taking in the air." To show he wasn't just kidding himself, he put his head out the window of his car and drew a deep breath. Immediately afterwards he looked at his fingernails to see if they'd grown.

The next moment he could not remember why he had done that. He had begun driving again. Ahead of him the sun was more than halfway down the sky, and now and then a hill or a

93

sudden dip in the road took it completely out of his view. If he had moments of nostalgia during those absences of the sun, he did not recognize them.

There was an iron gate across the road leading to the private beach. Behind the gate a boy in a baseball cap sat on a folding chair. When it did not seem as if the boy was going to rise, Shurnas started to get out of his car. Then he saw the boy had removed the baseball cap and was holding it out as if he expected him to put a tip in it. Shurnas took a quarter out of his pocket. When the boy said, "I couldn't hear you with the cap over my ears," Shurnas acted as if he'd only wanted to check the date on the quarter. He looked behind him to make sure no one else was within earshot. Still he could not bring himself to say the password aloud. So he whispered it. Eventually the boy got out of the chair and opened the gate. As Shurnas drove through it, the boy whispered, "They're all down there." Since Shurnas had started the whispering himself, he had some trouble convincing himself the words were a threat.

The road was deeply rutted. It came to an end at the edge of a high cliff overlooking the ocean. Some eight or ten cars were parked along the cliffline in a haphazard fashion that resembled the spokes of half a wheel. The image they made provoked the memory of a dream in Shurnas, and the memory of a dream provoked him to shudder as he got out of the car. When the shuddering continued he began paying more attention than usual to his surroundings as if looking for an omen that would tell him whether things were going to get strange again.

All at once he realized that the last four letters of the word women spelled omen; it seemed as if his only mistake awhile ago had been thinking in the singular! A winding footpath led down the side of the cliff. It didn't look unduly steep, but Shurnas found it forbidding all the same. He stood looking

94

down at the beach. Although there were still several hours of daylight left, the shadow cast by the cliff reached nearly to the edge of the water and he could see a faint outline of the moon low in the sky. Off to his right a volleyball game was in progress. From his vantagepoint the players looked like insects.

Nothing eventful happened when he took the footpath down the cliff. He didn't stumble, although the going was slippery in places and his back was still a little tender. The volleyball game didn't stop so that the players could stare at him as if he were an intruder, although his arrival meant there was now an extra man. The shadows on the beach didn't suddenly get longer, although it was growing later by the minute.

Each team had six players: three men and three women. Unwilling as he was to attach any significance to this, Shurnas could not escape the recognition that his presence had brought the total number of people there to thirteen. "A baker's dozen," he thought, glad that his was not the kind of mind that saw the gathering as Christ and his twelve disciples. When the game ended and he was asked if he had winners, it was another perfect moment. He knew no one there; no one knew him. So he introduced himself as William.

While the others were introducing themselves to him, Shurnas checked the measurements of the volleyball court by pacing off the distance between the orange ribbons that were being used to mark the boundaries. It puzzled him that one side of the court was several feet longer than the other. He asked a woman in a green bikini about the inequity and was told it was a way of compensating for the wind. There hadn't been any wind all day, but Shurnas didn't pursue the issue because, as a stranger here, he could hardly expect to impose his system of values on the others. Besides, a wind could come up at any moment, and wouldn't he look silly then?

Since someone had to sit out the next game in order for him to play, the six members of the losing team told him to pick a number between one and ten, then decided he would replace the person who came the closest to his number. Penalizing the one who made the best guess? Once again Shurnas felt his values were under attack. Mentally he chose three as his number, then quickly changed it to six. Realizing at all he'd done was double three, he thought, "No! It's eight!" But eight was no better because the shape of it was formed by the merger of two threes—one written backward and the other forward. In the end he settled on four and felt vindicated when no one guessed it. Although it was true of course that he'd cheated.

When Shurnas informed the others that four had been his number, it turned out that a man who had guessed three was the loser. So, in the real end, he'd accomplished nothing by changing his number. He was discouraged when the man who'd lost calmly spread a towel on the sideline and sat on it. He was further discouraged when another man slapped him on the back. In the face of all this camaraderie he had no choice now but to start thinking of himself as part of the group.

During the game his teammates kept shouting phrases like "attaway to go" at him. Each phrase was accompanied by a variation of William. Will. Willy. Bill. Billy. One woman even cried, "Good show, Willy-Billy!" Stirred by their enthusiasm, Shurnas began playing like a wild man. He dove headlong for balls. He leaped high over the top of the net to block "spike" shots with his forearms. He spiked the ball so hard himself at times that players on the opposing team began covering their heads with their hands whenever they saw him set himself to hit a shot.

His performance made the game so interesting that several passersby stopped to watch. One of them, a man in a white terrycloth robe, stood quietly to one side of the court puffing on a cigar. After a while he began offering humorous asides that compared Shurnas's talents to one famous athlete or another. His gargantuan leaps reminded the man of Wilt

Chamberlain. They way he smashed the ball was like Jimmy Connors. Ordinarily Shurnas would have been stimulated by all the attention, but something about the man disturbed him. Underlying the humor he seemed to hear a note of reproach in the man's voice.

When it came his turn to serve Shurnas ran off five straight points. The man was strangely quiet. After his next serve earned his team its sixth straight point, someone said he had a "streak" going. The man said something then. When he spoke Shurnas realized that the only reason he had identified him as a man was because he was smoking a cigar. His facial features were actually quite feminine, and who knew what lay underneath the terrycloth robe? Pretending his back was bothering him again, Shurnas deliberately hit his next serve into the net.

His streak was over. There would be no more comparisons now to "Pete Rose."

He wanted to tell himself he was in a trance, but he couldn't remember how it felt to be sure you were awake. He tried at least to remember when it had all started. He could not, finally, remember, but he was fairly certain it had been going on now for a long time. Then making himself repeat Pete Rose to himself brought him close to remembering something. The joke about Pete and Repeat; the novel, *A Rose Is a Rose Is a Rose*; and now the ballplayer who was going after DiMaggio's hitting-streak record. It wouldn't have taken too much for him to let his instinct to get out of there act for him. The others there were all looking at him. He started to stare back at them but then realized their faces were showing concern for him only because he was holding up the game. "Shake it off, Willy-Billy."

To prove he was not as helpless as all that, he mocked himself by shaking the arm that had made the bad serve. He noticed it was his right arm; in a dream, once you accepted that nothing was committed to happening logically, it could as

97

easily have been his left arm. So the possibility still existed that the strangeness was not imaginary. That realization alone ought to have panicked him. When it didn't he understood it must seem to him that the circle, so to speak, had been completed. He clapped his hands. The others on his team assumed he had recovered his spirit for the game and began shouting encouraging phrases at him again. Shurnas laughed. He was disappointed when nobody asked him why he was laughing.

When Shurnas's team won the game, they were immediately challenged to a rematch. Shurnas would have been wise to agree only on the condition that the boundaries were made equal on both sides of the court. In the tension of the game he had forgotten that one side was shorter than the other, and he looked now to see if it had been his team's side or his opponents' side. But the orange ribbons were hidden by all the sand that had been kicked over them in the course of the game. Also, most of the court was now in deep shadows. Here and there the faces of the others, in the fading sunlight, were indecipherable; the poles that supported the volleyball net seemed only extensions of the shadows; the net itself looked increasingly fuzzy.

Someone offered Shurnas a joint. He refused. Then he saw that the hand in front of him actually held two joints and he turned away, thinking, "Don't take gifts from strangers." Then he thought, "Never look a gift horse in the mouth." Which one applied here? Someone else said the fog was starting to come in. The person who spoke was already so indistinct to Shurnas that he did not realize at first that it was the woman who had called Willy-Billy. Out of the corner of his eye he seemed to see someone coming down the side of the cliff. But when he swung around the footpath was deserted.

For a time he continued to imagine someone was on the footpath. Then he saw that someone really was. He had not expected it would be a man. In a moment a woman in a sunhat appeared at the top of the cliff; when she started down the footpath behind the man, that was exactly what Shurnas had expected. "Here come Mr. and Mrs. A.C.-D.C.," the woman who had called him Willy-Billy said. Shurnas wondered how he could ever have thought all her playing on names was nonsense.

A new game started. The fog was rolling in so heavily that the ball couldn't be seen sometimes until it was right on top of you; after each point there would be an argument about whether or not the shot had landed in bounds. Each time Shurnas went for a ball his body seemed to begin right and then go awry. Even though he had refused the joints, it felt as if he had smoked them. As if all the fog in the air was marijuana. He thought he had better drop out of the game and instantly someone took his place although he hadn't made any signal that he was quitting. For a time he stood on the sideline; then he saw he was being watched by the woman in the sunhat. Between the fog and the loose-fitting cotton shift she wore he could see little of her but her eyes which stared at him like two pits from under the brim of the sunhat. She said nothing, just looked intently at him. It had all the elements of a contest, each of them waiting for the other to say the first word or make the first move. Shurnas wasn't about to do either one.

It was windy now. Shurnas went over to the cliff, let his eyes travel up the footpath to the top of it, and then began to climb. His back made it slow work. When he was halfway up the cliff, he turned around. The wind ruffled his hair. He saw the woman was following him; he stood motionless and watched her stop too and stand motionless. The temperature must have dropped because his body had a light chill over it. He climbed the rest of the way up the cliff, then turned around again. The woman was still following; in the fog he could see the shape of her sunhat coming along behind him.

Still watching over his shoulder, he walked very slowly to

his car. The woman seemed in no hurry either. In the car, he started the motor, then looked out the window and realized that he no longer saw her. But as he started to pull away, the door on the passenger's side was suddenly flung open and the woman jumped in. The angle of her sunhat kept him from seeing her face, but nothing spared him from hearing her voice. "Get me out of here," she said. "I'm bored out of my mind." It was definite that she sounded too husky to be Jackie, but it was also definite that in the country sounds traveled differently.

He put on his headlights. Even with them you could only see a few yards ahead of you. Not until they were on the Old Montauk Highway did he glance at the woman again. She still had the sunhat titled rakishly over her face, and that made him angry. He couldn't keep looking at her because he had to watch the road, and eventually his anger was transferred to the terrible conditions under which he had to drive. If the woman was a stranger he would have suggested they take a room for the night—at Gurney's Inn, say—but if the woman was who he was afraid she was that notion was futile. He kept waiting for her to introduce herself and at the same time was glad she didn't.

Meanwhile he counted the pairs of headlights that passed his car going in the opposite direction because they were the only distraction available in the fog. His eyes began to water. He was tired of having to stare into the distance ahead of him to avoid glancing at the woman beside him. At the same time he could hardly resist pulling the car off the road someplace and taking a look under that sunhat.

Though the fog was worsening, it was still daylight; the sun, wherever it was, would not begin to set for a while yet. In a few minutes, driving through the town of Montauk, he got a brief glimpse of it out toward the bay side, a pale yellow-white smear like a semen stain in the sky. He glanced at the woman's

100

profile, and the sudden violent yearning that came over him felt like a yearning to surrender himself once more and finally to whatever.

Still, he could not bear to listen to her voice. As though it had depressed him in advance and he had already heard it too often, he stared out the windshield while she told him that she and Ray had docked for the weekend at a marina motel called Snug Harbor. The word docked was obviously intended to convey more than one meaning, and he resented that the woman had been so indirect. He also did not care for her casual interjection of her husband's name into the conversation without having first established that this Ray was her husband. Altogether it seemed to him that her failure to speak to the point was just like a woman. Then he heard her say, "Oh Christ, when I saw your legs back there on the beach, I nearly creamed," and he thought he'd better not go jumping to any conclusions. He left Montauk behind him and headed east on the main highway. When she asked him where he was going, he said, "Just driving." In this fog? Maybe they could outrun it, he said. She told him not to be ridiculous; he'd have more luck trying to outrun his own shadow.

It had the feel of a domestic squabble. Shurnas could almost believe the woman was married to him and not to Ray. Then he realized that Ray, depending on how you spelled it, could also be a woman's name. "Who was that man with you on the beach?" he said. When she said, "You're my man now," he asked her if Rae was short for Rachel. At length, feeling her silence meant he was on the right track, he allowed himself to succumb to the gentle movements of the car as it rolled along the highway. His anger left him and he began to get pleasantly sleepy. It no longer mattered who the woman was. Soon it would be night, and in the dark all colors looked about the same and all people felt about alike.

The highway ended when they got to the lighthouse at the

tip of Montauk Point. A few hundred yards from the light-house station was an enormous parking area with a tollbooth at the entrance to it. The woman offered to pay whatever it cost to park just so he'd stop driving, but when they pulled up to the tollbooth there was no one in it. "You can't give money to a ghost," Shurnas said. He drove to a remote corner of the parking area and turned off the motor. After a while it began to get dark. Even though Shurnas could no longer see the fog, it was still there; the beam from the lighthouse, each time it swung through the sky, was so watery that it seemed he was looking up at it from the bottom of an ocean. "I can't decide whether nights like this are scary or romantic," the woman said. "How is there a difference?" Shurnas thought, but he said nothing.

Later on the woman walked down to the ocean and he fol-lowed her. Together they scrambled through coarse under-brush and over steep rocks. When they got to the beach, she immediately said, "Water, water everywhere but not a drop to drink," and he didn't have the heart to tell her that it was remarks like that that would decide him once and for all on who she was. After that, however, she stopped talking altogether. She didn't attempt to embrace him, she didn't so much as hold his hand, but Shurnas still sensed that she had led him down here for a purpose. And when at last she took off her sunhat and put it on a rock, he knew it was a signal that she was ready for him to start but felt as tentative as if he had been given a signal to wait. He was terrified by how deeply she stirred him, but in the next moment was stirred by how terrified of her he felt. When he realized her breathing had quickened his own grew very shallow, yet he felt as if he was panting.

As though she couldn't wait for him any longer, she put her arms around him and attempted to pull him down on top of her; and as though he had gone too fast she turned her head away and murmured for him to "cool it." Later she complained about his lack of experience, then said, "You make me feel positively virginal."

Shurnas tried to imagine that her face was still hidden by the sunhat, but the image was no longer successful. Whenever the beam from the lighthouse passed over them, he trembled for fear that her features would be illuminated. He lowered his head, eager to look into her eyes but at the same time closing his own. He caressed her in an effort to arouse her, then tore his hands away and put them behind his back. After touching him gently, she laughed and said roughly, "Look me up when your violet stops shrinking."

In a while she got on top of him and pantomimed the motions of intercourse without any part of her body making contact with his. "This sand's a killer," she said, and it reassured him to hear that he was not the only one feeling threatened. He swallowed so his voice wouldn't show too much relief, then told her his back was on the fritz. She said the reason she'd worn the sunhat was because she was afraid of getting skin cancer. He confessed that he hadn't eaten all day. She admitted she was still drinking too much. Her body was still pantomiming intercourse, but now, gradually, it had begun making contact with his. In a few moments he felt her settle down on him and realized that the fog had lifted because his eyes, still staring upwards over her shoulder, were dazzled by the full brilliance of the beam from the lighthouse.

All at once he smelled smoke. Lowering his eyes, he saw that the woman had lit a joint. "They were giving them away like candy at the volleyball game," she said. To himself Shurnas said, "So you took two," but the thought did not stop him from taking the joint from her. Where in the past he had been overcome by dread each time he was stricken by a sense of the familiar, at the moment he felt surprisingly calm. The notion that the circle had been completed was still uppermost in his mind. But then he remembered the appearance things had taken recently of beads on a necklace. As he puffed along on the joint, he murmured, "Politics and travel make strange bedfellows." Later he watched her light another joint and listened to her tell him that getting high after you balled was redundant.

They lay side by side on the sand like comrades and stared up at the moon.

When the woman fell asleep he secretly got dressed. She opened her eyes as he was putting his shoes on and told him to rub her back. With a yawn she rolled over on her stomach, Shurnas looked at her slender hips and buttocks, her skin took on the silver color of moonlight, he saw that she was asleep again. In a while, sitting up, he too fell asleep and woke himself intermittently with his own snoring. The tide came in, then went out. His eyes adjusted to the moonlight, then had to adjust to the darkness again when some clouds passed in front of the moon. While falling back to sleep he realized that the clouds were actually the beginning of another fog bank. He took a fleeting look at the woman; her skin now had a grayish cast to it.

Near dawn they made love a second time, sleepily, from a different angle. In the middle of it he thought of Ray or Rae in lonely wait for her in their room at the Snug Harbor and felt so sorry for that person that he grew very grave. Some other time he might have tried to express his sentiments to the woman, but now, taking an almost illicit pleasure in his own seriousness, he turned away from her so as to experience the moment more privately.

It was incredibly quiet on the beach. In front of the lighthouse the surf could be heard pounding against the rocks. Now and again a gull screeched. The woman was making moaning sounds as if trying to wake up from a bad dream. Nearby a boat was blasting its foghorn. Shurnas could almost imagine he was asleep.

Traces of the forthcoming dawn could be seen. You could watch the fog gradually getting lighter, as if someone was wiping off a very dirty window. What they said about fog having no color wasn't true. A lot of different varieties of gray could be seen, though none of them stood out enough to hold the eye in any one place. Shurnas had the feeling he might not even be awake.

He threw some rocks into the water. You saw them leave your hand, then had to listen for them to land before you could tell whether they had made it to the water. There was nothing much else to do in the fog. Between throws, realizing that he hadn't seen the woman in a while, Shurnas noticed that the beach was empty. He would have believed she had been washed out to sea, but when he looked at the rock where her sunhat had been it was empty too. It had been right then to come down to the water. You could bury your feelings, you could throw them to the wind, you could even burn them out of your mind, but never could you wash them away. As long as you were around water you were in a safety zone. Of course it helped if you thought all this out while you were half asleep because the condition of sleep was itself a safety zone. In those last few seconds before you dropped off everything was possible, including systems that never would have been allowed if you were awake.

It was too early yet for the tollbooth to be open when Shurnas went to get his car out of the parking area. He drove with his shoes unlaced, his socks in his shirt pocket. More and more he was beginning to look to himself as if he was on vacation. He played with the dials on the car radio until he got a station that was giving the news, listened to someone say they were bringing in a psychic to help in the hunt for the jogger killer, then hummed along to a tune that was used to introduce a commercial.

Shurnas knew he had no grounds now that he was wide awake for feeling as if a spell had been broken, but the fog had

105

a magical effect. Driving in it, you had to forget you were no longer asleep. So he did not step on the brake right away when the woman loomed in front of his car. She had the sunhat on again and the thumb of her right hand was cocked over her shoulder. The fog was so thick that he failed to see her face until the instant before the car hit her. Her mouth was open as if it wanted to tell him to make an exception to his rule about not picking up hitchhikers. But when he saw her eyes there was no way he could have. They came flaming at him from beneath the brim of the sunhat. If she had been a car they would have been her headlights blazing into the headlights of his own car. But through no one's fault but her own she wasn't a car. She was still Jackie.

He stopped the car and got out. This time there definitely should have been a lot to clean up. But the only thing he found when he went back to look was her sunhat. In the fog the rest of Jackie was lost. If was as if, in the impact with his car, she had evaporated. Nevertheless he had to keep looking for her because of the sunhat, because the sunhat was really there.

Little by little he thought of putting it on his own head. When he did his hair immediately felt like he needed a shower. Some time passed. Then Shurnas slowly returned to his car and examined the front end of it. To his disappointment he saw no damage. "That's the thing with these old cars," he told himself. "They were built to last." But the pinging sound was noticeably louder when he started the motor. For the first time Shurnas saw that in being concerned about what color things were he hadn't worried enough about how they sounded. He shook his head. It was true, what they were always saying, that a doctor was his own worst patient.

Since all the roads from Long Island led to New York, there was nowhere else to go. He was supposed to think that once he drove out of the fog he would see daylight, so it was natural, when he left the fog behind just outside of a town called Water

Mill, that the sky was black. There were even a few stars.

How the hell was he supposed to take that? What the devil was the significance of time never being what it was supposed to be afterwards? Why had it stopped surprising him that he was continually being surprised? Who was behind the game? What was it? Where was it? In him? Outside of him?

Shurnas knew he wasn't allowed to find the answers to any of these questions, but asking them kept him alert on the drive back. Since time was out of his control, he ought to concentrate on those things that were not. So he left his car on a side street on the Lower East Side of Manhattan with all the doors unlocked and the key dangling in the ignition. "Ditching the bitch," he thought, but as soon as he started walking away from the car he felt a pull in his chest that made him think he might be a little sad to see the old gal go. He went into a coffee shop and ignored the pay phone on the wall while he ordered ham and eggs. It was the middle of the night, and the place was deserted. The waitress, a young Puerto Rican girl, would have invited him to come home with her after she got off work, but Shurnas had anticipated her so far in advance that he said, "No way," to her before she could even smile at him. Later some Puerto Rican men came in for a take-out order of coffee and doughnuts. They were having an all-night poker game, one of them told Shurnas. A policeman entered the coffee shop. Shurnas, seeing a different message in each detail of his uniform, understood that he had been commanded to participate in the poker game and left with the men.

Because the neighborhood was dangerous all of the men carried knives in their hands as they walked along the street. They put them away when they got to a burned-out building. To Shurnas the prospect of spending the night in masculine activity outweighed the unsavory appearance of the building. He climbed the stairs behind the other men. When he got to the fifth floor, he was greeted by a man in an undershirt who said, "No heat, chief," and then yanked the sunhat off his head and threw it down the stairs.

The first room you saw when you entered the apartment was the kitchen. In the center of it was a big wood table. Shurnas waited for the other men to seat themselves around the table, then took the only vacant chair that was left. He reached for his wallet, but someone told him his money was no good here. Shurnas said, "What do you play for, matchsticks?" and reached for his wallet again. The man who had spoken to him grabbed his arms and swore at him in Spanish. Then someone else explained to Shurnas that strangers were only permitted to watch. Shurnas, who was just there for the companionship anyway, wasn't about to object. He got up to use the bathroom, but when someone asked him where he was going, he lied and said he had to make a phone call. Since there were obviously no phones in a place like this, he was not challenged.

The bathroom was down the hall. Shurnas had no particular errand there, but he closed the door behind him all the same. In case anyone was listening, he ran the water awhile in the sink. What he really wanted was a shower, and it was just unfortunate that he, a stranger, had no way of earning that privilege.

When he got back to the kitchen, the game was breaking up. Many of the men had already gone. As the rest were leaving, one of them informed Shurnas that it was his turn to clean up. Since this order was given to him in English, he suspected it had another meaning. When he turned around a middle-aged woman in a wrinkled housecoat was standing in the kitchen doorway. Her face at one time might have been pretty. She smiled at him and opened her housecoat to show him that she was wearing nothing under it. Shurnas did not have to be a genius to realize that being in the country had destroyed his ability to spot a set-up.

The woman started to mop the kitchen table with a wet rag. Shurnas did not really believe that he would be able to get out of there if he helped her clean up, but it was better than staring at her. A roach crawled across the floor. Shurnas, who was about to step on it, became more admiring of the woman when she screamed. Then he saw she wasn't screaming at the roach but at him for thinking of stepping on it. She said something to him in Spanish. He answered her with a shrug. In a while she sat down at the kitchen table, picked up a deck of cards that had been left behind by the poker players and dealt a hand of solitaire. Shurnas caught her cheating several times, but she still lost.

When a voice was heard elsewhere in the apartment the woman left the kitchen. At first Shurnas thought she had gone to take care of a child that had awakened. He sat down at the kitchen table and dealt himself a poker hand just to see how his luck would have run had he been allowed to play. He wound up with three queens. Scared, he threw them away. Then he grew angry at himself for letting superstition force him to break up a winning hand. The woman returned and stood in the kitchen doorway. Shurnas followed her into a back room. She threw off her housecoat and lay down on a bed that had no sheets or blankets, only a bare mattress. It was too late when Shurnas saw the TV set; he could no longer pretend the voice he'd heard had come from somewhere else. "We fly at dawn." He looked and looked at the TV screen, and eventually he realized the reason he saw no picture on it was because the screen was broken. Other furnishings in the room were in no better shape. A dresser with two drawers missing, holes in the window curtains, newspapers stuffed in the window itself. In these circumstances a fan or an air conditioner would have looked out of place, but he nevertheless refused to believe it when he did not see one.

Later the woman fell asleep and he lay down beside her so quietly that she did not stir. He left his clothes on, all except for his shoes. The voice from the TV set was so much like having another person in the room with you that he soon had an erection. When he penetrated the sleeping woman, however, he went limp instantly. Then he saw the window curtain was moving as if something was blowing it. An air conditioner, after all?

After a while the woman grew more or less aware of his presence. She never actually woke up, but he noticed that each time the window curtain moved she murmured something in Spanish.

CHAPTER SIX

All night his whole body was suffused with a feeling of impending doom which did not leave him until the woman got up to turn on the TV set. Then he began to stir restlessly in his sleep and woke up feeling tired. His clothes were in a heap on the floor and cooking smells came from the kitchen. Beside him the mattress was empty. In a short while the woman returned, and so did the feeling of doom.

He pulled back the curtain but did not try to look out the window. The newspapers stuffed in the holes in the pane were too much of an obstacle; you didn't have to see the headlines on them to know they had been put there to taunt you. When he picked up a magazine and began fanning himself with it, the woman made hand gestures that told him all his arm motions were making her dizzy. When she went on making hand gestures after he'd put the magazine down, he thought she must be insane. But he stopped believing that when he remembered the guilty look on her face when he'd caught her cheating at solitaire. As if she had known right from wrong.

It did not occur to him that the hand gestures were her way of overcoming the language barrier between them until he had to make some of his own to get her to understand he needed a shower. That reminded her—she had left water boiling on the stove. Shurnas watched her trundle off down the hall. When he had dressed and gone into the kitchen, he watched her hands tell him to sit down at the table. His own hands had nothing more to say, so he just sat there with them in his lap. After a while he saw her head motion in the direction of the bathroom: did he still want a shower? It did him no good to shake his own head no because his earlier hand gestures had already committed him.

While he was in the shower the woman came into the bathroom and made hurryup motions with her hands. She left the door ajar so he could hear her banging pots and pans around in the kitchen. After he had joined her at the table, her hands, her head, everything about her was quiet, but he held no hope that would last. On the table in front of him was a steaming cup of coffee and nothing else. All that noise for just *this?* When he had stared into his coffee cup awhile, he could imagine the woman was no longer there. And when he heard her voice talking to him in Spanish, he tried to imagine he only imagined that. On the floor between his feet lay a chewing gum wrapper. The woman wasn't chewing gum and neither was he, so it was conceivable that they were not alone.

The woman was telling him that she had to go to the hospital for an operation. Some female problem. The moment she set foot outside the door of her apartment a marshal would seize it since the building was condemned and no one was supposed to be living there. Shurnas did not have to be told that he had to guard the apartment. Though he spoke no Spanish, he understood the woman perfectly. It was as if the person there with them who was chewing gum was acting as an interpreter.

She went into the back room to pack a bag; when Shurnas arrived she opened the door of the closet. She seemed to do it without thinking, and he seemed to know what he would see without looking. Still his eyes kept threatening to slip away from him while she was dressing and glance into the closet. Finally he said, "I can't stay here!" Before the woman could answer him he shouted, "There's nothing for me to wear!" She made some hand gestures as if she understood, but then *he*

112

understood she only wanted his help in zipping up her dress.

The moment she turned her back to him he hastily closed the closet door. As soon as she left he secretly washed out the clothes he was wearing in the kitchen sink so that he wouldn't have to feel he needed clean ones. While he was waiting for them to dry, he did some exercises. It seemed to Shurnas that he had not been trying hard enough to stay in shape. His body was literally beginning to get away from him. To prove his point he got down on the floor in a pushup position and pretended his arms were too weak to support him. When he realized he was naked, he pretended the cords of flesh he saw everywhere he looked weren't muscles but flab. While jumping up and down on his toes he kept his hands cupped protectively over his breasts and pretended he felt a weightless sensation between his legs.

In a few minutes, although his clothes were still quite wet, he got dressed and went out to . . . to do what? He soon got tired of walking around the neighborhood because every place he went looked like a place he had already been. From time to time he stopped in a store, but since he no longer had a mustache it did not count when none of the clerks recognized him. Or had he grown a mustache so he would not be recognized? Shurnas saw that he was in danger of becoming ridiculous. Already, ridiculously, his exposed face was perspiring from walking around in the hot sun while his body had a chill from walking around in wet clothes.

Ahead of him Shurnas saw a small park. As there were no trees in it, only a few benches, he wondered what had made him conclude it was a park. But then, a few steps farther on, he saw a sign on the iron fence behind the benches: "No ballplaying in the park." So his conclusions were still shared on occasion by others. A young mother sat on one of the benches. He did not have to ask himself for written proof that she was a mother because there was a naked child playing on the ground at her feet. The size made it a child. That the child had a penis made it a boy. Of course the penis could be artificial, the child could have been a midget and the mother could have been a passerby who'd merely sat down next to it to rest—but once you started looking for tricks in every little thing, where were you?

Shurnas sat down on the bench right beside the mother, even though she did not make room for him. He told her his pants were wet because he'd just washed them, even though she was looking at his face. Then he told her it was too hot for mustaches, even though her eyes had dropped to his pants.

In a while the mother took a diaper out of her purse, wrapped it around the child and stood up as if to leave. Shurnas had just remembered there was a reason for sitting down beside her. By the way, he said, did she know where Eldridge Street was? When the mother sat down again, it seemed to Shurnas that between the iron fence behind the benches and the wet clothes he was wearing he had unwittingly imprisoned himself. Still he did not get unduly nervous when she pointed over his shoulder and said, "A block or so back the way you just came from."

Must not have been watching, he said. Did she mean the street where it looked as if there'd been a fire?

When the mother did not answer right away, Shurnas thought he would surprise her by saying, "You know, the one where that woman was killed." But instead he crossed his legs as if to make this a leisurely conversation. For just a second he believed that to anyone watching him sit there with a mother and her child, he could not possibly look as if he were guilty of anything. Against that impression, however, was the one he made of someone who knew the neighborhood. So now, wasn't it better to disassociate himself from the mother and child?

The mother had said there'd been a fire on her own street

114

just last week. Shurnas, acting as if he were the one surprised by the turn the conversation had taken, said, "In the summer?" Many fires occurred in the summer, the mother told him; people were careless year around. Shurnas gave her what he thought was the perfect opening when he said maybe, but had she ever known of one in the summer where anybody was killed?

"Death doesn't care what season it is," she said.

Thinking there was a lie if he'd ever heard one, Shurnas waited for her to tell him about the fire on Eldridge Street. Instead she shook her finger at the child and told it not to dirty itself. So Shurnas had to be the one, after all, who said, "The only way to fight fire is with fire." It was just about the only advice you could give that was good the world over, but the effect it had was to make the child start crying. As if it still wanted to believe differently. "Did you make pooh-pooh?" the mother said to it. To Shurnas she said, "It never fails. As soon as you change them, they go." In a less conversational tone Shurnas said, "What about Eldridge Street?" But the mother was suddenly too busy putting another diaper on the child to look up.

Later he noticed that the burned-out building was not on Eldridge Street. Although he should have been relieved, he grew irritated. Now it was not going to be so easy to find out what he had been doing on Eldridge Street. There was a post office nearby. He entered it and stood awhile at the end of a long line, then moved to another line that seemed to be moving faster. At the window he was told that he'd have to stand on the first line again for the information he wanted. To beat the system, he called the post office from a pay phone across the street and was told that he'd have to appear in person to get that kind of information; even then it was unlikely they'd have a Change-of-Address card on file that had been submitted so long ago. Since Shurnas still had the envelope that had been

115

forwarded from Eldridge Street, it angered him that he was not allowed simply to go to the address on it. Why did they always have to make everything so complicated?

As he walked along the street, a man in front of him tossed a newspaper into a trash basket. He had so much experience in seeing objects that stuck straight up in the air like a sail that he automatically read the headline even as he was automatically turning his head away from it. The psychic had declared that the jogger killer was a man who hated women who hated men. Since the damage had already been done, he took the newspaper out of the trash basket and glanced through the rest of it. The Yankees and Red Sox had both won; a bride in Connecticut was filing for an annulment because her husband had revealed on their wedding night that he was a clone; some joggers on the Montauk Highway had stumbled on the body of a young man who was an apparent hit-and-run victim.

Shurnas leaned against the side of a building and folded the newspaper so it would look to people who passed him as if he was pondering the entries in the harness races that night. Had the man who'd thrown the newspaper away intended it to fall into his hands? If you believed that—and what choice did you have?—was the story about the hit-and-run victim a plant? He looked again at the page where he'd seen the story and though it looked no different than all the rest of the pages in the newspaper, he could see where they would know exactly how to put it together so he would be fooled.

The crossword puzzle had even been finished, to give the appearance the man was really done with the newspaper when he threw it away. And the bridge hand had been torn out. It was small details like that that told you the whole thing was a put up job. Was he under surveillance right this minute? Shurnas, having played in enough tennis tournaments to know how to handle himself under pressure, laughed as if he'd just read something that amused him. Before tossing the news-

116

paper back into the trash basket, he was careful to open it to the comic section.

Nevertheless he was followed into the burned-out building by two policemen. They stayed well behind him on the stairs until he got to the fifth floor. Even there they waited for him to open the door of the women's apartment before revealing themselves. While one of them posted himself between Shurnas and the stairs, the other one said, "Where's the woman?" Their uniforms alone—never mind the guns!—were too much for him. "The jig is up," he heard himself think. They steered him into the apartment, told him to sit down at the kitchen table and then closed and locked the door. The one who'd asked him where the woman was now said, "Where's the key?" Shurnas realized the question was legitimate, although it would have made more sense coming from him.

He noticed as he was taking his wallet out of his pocket that the lining inside the pocket still felt damp. Actually, let's face it, his pants weren't dry yet. Would they think, when they saw the condition he was in, that he'd wet himself out of nervousness? He crossed his legs so that the dampness between them, in the event there was some, wouldn't show. As he handed over his wallet, the pupils of the eyes of the policeman who took it widened, but there was nothing noticeably accusatory in them. The movement Shurnas made to settle back in his chair gave him an opportunity to glance down the hall of the apartment. Thankfully, the closet door in the back room was still closed.

The policeman who was looking through Shurnas's wallet said that he was a trespasser unless he could prove he was a relative of the woman's. After a while Shurnas understood he was being offered a chance to make a "clean breast" of his role in the jogger murders. Though he loathed the allusions raised by such expressions, he could accept that they had a place in police work. Might as well confess, he said. "You've got me cold." With a curt nod the policeman returned his wallet to him. The other policeman had already opened the door, with the comment that he had twenty-four hours to get out of the building. Shurnas watched them go, then quickly locked the door behind them. Their feet went down the stairs. When Shurnas tried to look through the peephole, he saw that some-one had stuck a piece of chewing gum in it. He thought about recent events and decided that no matter how you added them up he had been pardoned. He took off his clothes and after spreading them on the kitchen table to finish drying, went into the back room to lie down.

The closet door remained closed all afternoon. Shurnas hardly took his eyes off it, although for a moment here and there he probably fell asleep. Around dusk he went out to a delicatessen for a pastrami sandwich and had it wrapped "to go" so he could continue to watch the closet door while he ate it. When he returned to the burned-out building, the moon was out; it looked blue, which wasn't too bad considering there were songs that said it was at times. As he entered the building, some kids of all different colors were playing on the front stoop. He did not look down because he did not want to have to acknowledge them. "The child is the father of the man." Outside the building he might have gotten away with thinking that was just a clever turn of phrase on someone's part, but now that he was going indoors again he no longer had that freedom.

Since it was getting dark earlier these days, the baseball game hadn't started yet when he turned on the TV set. At one point while he was eating his sandwich the closet door got very close to him and either the mattress underneath him or the ceiling above him narrowed the distance between them. But when he closed his eyes it no longer felt like a life or death proposition. To find out whether the shrinking had been per-manent he flung his arms out to the sides as far as they could reach, then stretched them high over his head. He touched nothing; nothing touched him. Shurnas found it hopeful to be able to learn this by using his body; it meant he could still treat himself as if he were real.

It was quiet lying there; the voice on the TV set wasn't talking to him. He could go to sleep any time. He lay still in the growing darkness; all at once, when he was almost asleep, he felt panicked because his car was gone. Something had been taken away from him, had left a terrible void now in his life. He didn't want to have to remember that he'd put it there himself. Aloud to himself he said, "What have I lost?" It woke him up. Since he had been dreaming when he spoke, he did not have to answer himself. He nearly couldn't stand it any more that every time he turned around he was being pardoned.

When he awakened the next morning it was already blazing hot. Though he still had some time before his twenty-four hours was up, he left the burned-out building without lingering to shower, shave or eat. He spent the morning walking downtown to the Battery and back uptown to Houston Street. Time and again during his walk it felt as if someone else was moving for him, acting as his stand-in. He had heard that people lost contact with themselves after an upheaval in their lives; leaving his ex-wife must have been the wrench that was thrown into the works, he decided. Or had she left him? It was also still possible to believe at times that he had never been married.

He took the "F" train to West 23rd Street, sitting in the last car so he wouldn't have as far to walk to 19th Street after he got out. Remembering that his ex-wife liked to paint outdoors in the summer, he did not waste time going to her place but headed immediately toward the river. On the way two joggers passed him and he caught himself running a little himself, although who was in a hurry? Then he saw one of the joggers looked like his ex-wife. With her was a woman in a red T-shirt that had the number "86" painted on the back. Shurnas did not know whether to catch up to the two women. That you got eight by merging a backwards and a forwards three meant one thing; that you got six by doubling three meant another. Likewise, three was a crowd on the one hand, but on the other hand there had been three wise men and three musketeers. When he got within sight of the river, the two women were only a few yards ahead of him. They were deep in conversation; now and then, as they ran side-by-side, their elbows brushed against each other. Shurnas saw that he was too late. "She's like all the others now," he thought.

At the intersection of Tenth Avenue and 23rd Street a gypsy cab picked him up. The driver was wearing a black beret. The cab must have needed work because there was a pinging noise in the motor. As if it were a tune running through his head, Shurnas sat in the back seat drumming his fingers on his knee. There was so much traffic that the cab couldn't go anywhere. That was all right with Shurnas; for the moment he'd gone about as far as he wanted to anyway. Once in a while he'd forget that the cab reminded him of his car; then he'd stop drumming his fingers and remember it again. The color was different, but colors had a way of changing very quickly in this weather. "It's as if the sky is snowing blood." Shurnas didn't ask the driver if he'd found the car on the street, painted it red and stuck a meter on the dashboard; his only question was whether the old gal could ever forgive him.

At first the driver was patient with the heavy traffic, but soon he began to get angry. Shurnas didn't want any hassles when he was feeling so nostalgic. Suddenly the driver spotted an opening in the next lane and cut in front of a Volkswagen Rabbit. The man driving the Rabbit stuck his fist out the window and shook it. That, reasonably, should have been the end of the incident, but at the next light Shurnas was given a jolt when the Rabbit pulled up alongside the cab and both drivers got out and started pushing each other.

Because things that didn't involve you had a way of involving you, Shurnas looked the other direction. Thus he didn't realize the two men were wrestling on the hood of the Rabbit until a policeman pounded on the door of the cab. Stop rubber-necking, the policeman shouted, and get this car out of here so traffic can move. Shurnas would have said the bitch wasn't his, but he was too afraid, if it ever came down to it, plenty of proof could be found that she was. He jumped behind the wheel. At the next light a man carrying a bright red patent leather tennis bag got into the back seat and told Shurnas to take him to the tennis courts in Central Park. And step on it!

The meter on the dashboard kept skipping numbers, maybe from a short circuit caused by the pinging in the motor. By the time they got to Columbus Circle it already registered nine dollars. The man in the back seat said it was a three-dollar trip and if Shurnas tried a rip-off, there'd be trouble. Shurnas glanced into the rearview mirror, but the man's eyes were too eager to meet his and he looked out the windshield again. Traffic on Central Park West was bad; the man said he should have taken Amsterdam Avenue, what kind of a game was he running? There was a document of some sort on the front seat. Thinking it was a message for him, Shurnas picked it up. It was the car title he thought he'd thrown out with the key to the woman's apartment on York Avenue.

On the dashboard behind the meter was a piece of paper that stuck straight up in the air like a sail; beside it, taped to the dashboard in a neat row, were some half a dozen keys. Shurnas had driven long enough to know how easy it was to have an accident if you let things distract you. He did not look twice when he saw a pile of clothes on the floor of the car. He did not have to look twice: those clothes hadn't been sent to the cleaners for no reason.

The door of the glove compartment was open; crammed inside were a magazine, some newspapers, and protruding out of the clutter, the toes of a pair of blue running shoes.

That pair of shoes —

So little of what Shurnas saw made sense to him, and there was so little to see that could not be made to make sense to him.

Was he still defended on all fronts?

That possibility was so intolerable that it was quickly washed away by a panic that came almost as a relief. He grabbed the piece of paper that stuck straight up in the air like a sail, made a paper airplane out of it and threw it out the window. There would be hell to pay when they found it. Of course now that it was no longer shaped like a sail it would no longer read like an indictment.

Had he just granted himself another pardon?

It was so quiet in the car that the pinging in the motor grew louder and louder like somebody's stomach rumbling from not being fed enough. At the next intersection children were crossing the street in single file behind a woman who had the look of a teacher; a man who was wearing a doorman's uniform but had the look of a foreign premier was signaling for a cab. Driving on, he saw a dog that didn't look like anything but a dog. Wasn't that nature's fault?

At the 96th Street entrance to the park the man muttered that all of Shurnas's scheming to jack up the fare had made him late for his match, then pushed some bills into Shurnas's hand and got out. Shurnas pulled the cab into a parking place that his watch told him was illegal for another ten minutes yet. It would serve the bitch right if she was towed away. Then he remembered it had not been her idea to have the meter put in.

"It takes two to tango," he thought, meanwhile wondering if he could ever feel the same about the old gal now that she'd started doing it for money.

He was still there in conflict when he saw the man come running out of the park. Anticipating trouble, he tried to start the motor, but the man opened the door and grabbed the key out of the ignition. Shurnas shouted for him to keep his hands to himself. The man pocketed the key and shouted that to get it back Shurnas would have to fill in for his regular partner who'd gotten another game when he was late. Shurnas immediately said he didn't have his tennis racket with him, thinking he had the perfect out. But when the man said, "You can use my spare," it occurred to him that one man's meat didn't necessarily have to be another man's poison.

He got out of the cab. It was exactly the hour. The wench was safe now from being towed away. "You're on your own," he told her. "Don't take any wooden nickels while I'm gone."

On the walk to the tennis courts Shurnas saw, between himself and the man who, walking ahead of him, had just crossed the bridle path, a long stream of joggers passing as if in review. All of them wore shoes so new they looked as if they'd been painted on their feet. Every pair was blue, a color that had become very popular of late. Shurnas had to wait until the joggers went by before he could cross the bridle path, so he tended to notice them in detail. Were those bulges under their T-shirts guns? Slipping now and then in the cinders, he hurried after the man. He didn't look back.

In the clubhouse the man explained that unless he had a parks department tennis permit he would have to buy a single-play ticket. "It's a crazy system," the man said. Shurnas, who found it entirely sensible, nevertheless walked out on the courts as though in a strange element. When the man fished his spare racket out of his tennis bag, Shurnas instantly put the racket in his left hand. The air was hazy, the shimmering sun

123

lurked just overhead. During the warmup Shurnas continued to move as though in a strange element, as though in someone else's body. It was astonishing how different things felt when you did them lefthanded. After a while he had to rest; the other side of his body simply wasn't accustomed to being used. He tried to look for an image of himself in himself as he usually looked for an image of himself outside himself, to tell him what to do. But it was still too soon for that. When you fought fire with fire, the wires could get pretty crossed up.

Then the man was telling him they ought to play for a new can of balls just to make their match interesting. By that time Shurnas had seen enough to know the man was an awful player; he was so awful that Shurnas's embarrassment at being on the same court with him made him think of two drowning men in the middle of the ocean. After each point Shurnas had to restrain himself from looking at the man with pity. He was wearing auburn shorts that were too big for him and a sun visor with fingermarks on it. His hands were perspiring so much that he kept igniting a cigarette lighter and holding his racket handle over the flame to dry it. Shurnas, who was playing in streetclothes, was sweating more than a little himself; doing things with your left hand really was like having them done by somebody else. Once, at game–point, he hit a serve that was long by two feet. The man bent over the spot where the ball had landed for a long time, then rose up and stiffly announced it was good. "When in doubt, you can't call it out," he said. Since this attitude toward the world was the direct opposite of the one the man had taken in the cab, Shurnas had no notion of what his own attitude should be. What were other men anyway if they weren't adversaries? He tried to repeat his first impression of the match: "Two drowning men in the middle of the ocean." But it kept on being tennis until his foot began to hurt.

It was the foot on his right leg.

Later Shurnas missed an easy shot, only to be told to play the point over because somebody had walked behind the court in the middle of it.

Some clouds had come within range of the sun, though none of them as yet could manage to get in front of it; the heat was still unrelieved. Shurnas had a cramp now in his foot and couldn't get rid of it.

He missed another easy shot. From across the net he heard the man tell him to play the point over; that fire engine, in the distance, must have been a distraction. The man's voice was so accommodating that listening to it made his head ache.

It was not going to be easy. There were contests between men, and then there were contests between men. But this had the feel of a new one on him.

Shurnas shifted from good foot to bad foot, helpless and confused. He hit a serve into the fence, it bounced off and clipped the man in the back of the head, the fence rattled. The man pursed his lips, then told Shurnas to take the serve over because all the bounding around the ball had done had caused a delay.

Shurnas walked up and down; the man merely stood patient, still and waiting. Finally the sun went behind a cloud. A new picture appeared on the court: the man took off his sun visor and tossed it aside. He dried off his racket handle with the cigarette lighter, then motioned to Shurnas that he was ready again.

Shurnas stared at the cloud until it passed. The moment the sun emerged again, he served with the racket in his right hand. Blinded, the man made no attempt to return the ball. Was it in or out? he asked. When Shurnas shrugged as if to say it was the man's decision to make, things began to feel as if they were going to get back to normal. He could begin to follow in his own mind the interplay of the systems again, and it was he himself who once more controlled the logic of them. It was of his own free will that he was returning to being a puppet in the hands of fate. Using the wrong hand, consciously, he had almost let himself become a quarterback who called his own game, but the sun had given him back his sense that he was getting his signals from the coach, so to speak.

The man could not go on hesitating forever. Eventually he had to say something. At last his teeth unclenched and he did.

"Out," he shouted. "What you can't see, you can't believe."

As if that were all he had been waiting to hear, Shurnas turned and walked off the court.